der wald

der wald

Benjamin Gardner

Adorcist Books

One

The first phantom vision I remember was a strange one. It was a great tree, an old tree standing in the middle of the forest, given plenty of room by the other plants of the forest to grow. Blue bottles hung from it, even in the highest branches, and the heads of dolls and toys rested at each intersection of branch with trunk. The image itself pulsed and moved as if the tree would uproot and walk towards me at any moment.

These types of visions didn't happen often. My doctor said there was a name for it, some kind of syndrome I've forgotten now, but I'd always thought of it as phantom vision, similar to cases of people who had pain or other sensations in limbs that no longer existed. Dr. Hoffmann told me true phantom vision was usually found in older people who had lost their sight, but I thought about the things I saw like a missing limb. I knew they were hallucinations, because most of them were disjointed and didn't make sense—but they were real enough that they seemed like something that used to be mine. I suppose my brain still wanted to see things even though my eyes no longer could.

Waiting in the theater to attend *Der Wald* with Jefre, I had another vision. People were just taking their seats when I saw my hands holding a gun. At first, I thought it was related to a hunting trip with my stepfather, but then I realized the context was all wrong. I was holding a rifle, pointing it at something in the shadows. I was up high, but not as high as a tree stand. I was on horseback, and my gun was trained on dark figures standing in a field.

I reflexively rubbed my eyes, then touched everything around to regain my sense of reality. It didn't usually make the hallucination go away, but it sometimes helped me settle down. The image jumped around and then began to fade, a fuzzy projection of a thought lodged somewhere in my brain.

Everyone in the theater got quiet—they must have dimmed the lights. I could only hear the rustling of programs and bodies adjusting in the velveteen seats.

"I wish Hana could be here with us," I whispered to Jefre.

"I know." It was a diplomatic response. He was used to my comments about her, but I could feel the tension in his shoulders, the sleeves of his rough tweed blazer moving as his posture changed.

Hana and I met when we were in college, and I'd met Jefre soon after. I really loved both of them and, after dating Jefre for some time and deciding together that we were better as friends, Hana and I started spending more and more time together. Before long we were married, living our lives together, and then she was just gone. After she left, Jefre called at least once a week to see how I was doing. We started spending more time with one another again.

I leaned over to say something else but Jefre cut me off. "It's about to start," he said.

The silence just before the performance made the theater feel monolithic. I suddenly thought of a cartoon of Jonah, surrounded by cathedral-like bones inside a whale. I'd always loved this theater, but somehow the space inside of it had turned slightly bitter, until I heard the opera start.

The first songs involved three females, one a soprano voice. Though I didn't catch everything, they seemed to be a group of nymphs that lived in trees discussing the ephemerality of all things human.

"Would you like me to describe what's happening?" Jefre whispered.

"I just want to listen," I whispered back.

One of the things about opera is that it is like a gate. I don't always catch everything that's being spoken, but something about the combination of the libretto and music opens up something in me, a doorway to a whole different side of my consciousness. I did not imagine the dryads talking about these things but I understood it to be so, thanks to this other part of my consciousness that wasn't available except during arias.

It is also a place of contemplation for me. I reckoned the tree nymphs were performing some kind of ritual amongst the trees on stage, perhaps around an altar. They were singing of three generations of humans who had passed away, and they looked upon us with pity, crooning of the brevity of the lives and the problems of people.

One of the voices sounded like Hana's. I loved to hear her sing the "Flower Duet" and, whoever this soprano was, she transported me back to a rainy day in Hana's apartment when she sang the soprano part. I touched Jefre's elbow on the armrest between us and asked him who was singing.

He told me the name, but I forgot it almost immediately. It wasn't Hana, even though I desperately wanted it to be - to know that she was alive and singing and that I was here to hear it once more. I was transfixed on the swirling voices chanting the nymphs' rituals, tangling me up in a trance-web in the trees of the wood where I'd stay until a spider devoured me. I held that somber and beautiful image - of me being emptied out and left as a husk wrapped in the web of a spider - as the singing continued.

I could sense the room spinning. I was glad to have the fold-down seat of the old theater but it couldn't hold me as I was taken in with the hypnotic silk of the sounds coming from the stage. I worried that Jefre would find me on the floor, limp and twisted beneath the seats.

From what little I knew about the opera, this part wasn't supposed to last this long. It seemed to go on for an age; the sopranos' song morphing into a drone oscillating around some grand reality. I was in awe of what was happening but knew I would not be able to remember everything, so I tried to listen.

And then, abruptly, it ended. I waited for the next part of the opera, but it never came. The theater was silent. I reached for Jefre's shoulder and there was nothing there. He wasn't on either side of me and I suspected that no one else was there, either. The theater felt empty.

"Hello?" I was hesitant and quiet, in case I'd just become confused, or gripped by a particularly powerful phantom vision. I took out my cane for some sense of place.

No one answered except the echo of my own voice. Then the operatic ritual of the wood nymphs began to fade in, their singing filling the empty theater, except that it was distant. The singing was no longer coming from the stage.

I corrected the strange angle that my body had descended to and stood up, holding the seat in front of my own. I felt the backs of the seats as I made it to an aisle and started to try and find my way to an exit.

The slope of the aisle flattened and soon I could feel a door, but it was locked.

Something churned deep inside me, the belly of the theater swallowing any sense of orientation. The emptiness of the building started growing inside of me, a void from my stomach branching up fed by fear and dread.

I thought I heard something towards the stage so I stopped and turned towards it. It was an odd sound that didn't belong - something like a tree frog or crickets in the distance. It didn't return.

I stepped back towards the seats and slowly made my way toward the stage. As I got closer a remarkable thing happened; the temperature grew a few degrees cooler. The sounds of insects grew louder but remained distant, as if separated by glass.

I found the stage eventually and used my hands to guide myself to the stairs. I walked up the stairs and braced myself against the decorative molding on the side of the stage. The wood was textured like tree bark, which I thought odd.

"Hello?"

I walked onto the stage and tapped around. There was no set or curtain at all. An image came to my mind of a giant film projection screen. From the seats it looked pitch black, but now I was walking in it, proving (to an empty house) that the flat black rectangle had another dimension. I could see it in my head as plain as day. I was walking in an empty flat black rectangle and I was alone.

I could still hear singing and the sounds of insects, though muffled, as if a bell jar covered them, but the smells around me were powerful and unmistakable: earthy and damp, like a forest just after a rain.

As I searched for anything in this strange place that would have pointed to a rational explanation of what was happening, I found a chair next to the heavy stage curtain. I felt a headache dancing at my temples and sat down. I rubbed my eyes again, trying to make sense of what was happening.

+++

The second I closed my eyes, I saw it. I saw the forest. I saw the ground, the space between the trees, the insects buzzing in the air, the birds flitting from branch to branch. I was sitting on a felled tree, not a folding chair.

I'm not saying that I imagined it—that hearing some distant sound of insects and smelling the dampness of the forest floor made me conjure a phantasm of the forest. I mean that I could *see* the forest. I was in it.

But only when my eyes were closed. When I opened my eyes I was again without sight, sitting on a folding chair in a blank space. A flat black rectangle you could actually walk around in.

Trying hard to keep my eyes closed, I stood up from the felled tree and walked through the woods. I touched the bark on each tree, seeing if what I had experienced as an empty space really held old-growth trees. I picked off a piece of a shagbark hickory and held it in my hand. I could see the forest, walk through it, and touch every part.

After a couple of hundred steps I opened my eyes. Instantly I was back in my own blinded vision that I was used to, but could feel the strange stage, the void.

"Hello?" Again, there was no answer.

I closed my eyes and I was where I'd left off in the woods, leaning against the massive trunk of a great oak tree.

Opened, there was an absence of vision but the smell and feeling of the old theater. Hollow sounds of an empty stage, but somehow different than the belly of the whale that I felt as an audience member.

I could still hear the songs of the nymphs, further and further away. Their lyrics spoke of two worlds that I couldn't help feeling I was in the middle of, unfurling between two impossible places. I had no idea which reality was better—or indeed if both or either were real. I had no understanding whatsoever of what had just happened.

T W O

Walking through the forest, eyes closed, was awkward at first; I felt like I should have my cane, and the ground moved unnaturally. Years ago, still sighted, I experienced the same sensation when my eyeglass prescription changed; the world around me would feel detached and I would step carefully. Now I gradually became more comfortable and learned how to negotiate my body through the trees.

The forest floor was covered in vining green plants and leaves. Parts were patchy with undergrowth and other areas had flattened to nothing but rust-colored pine needles. I walked slowly and stopped often, taking in all the details of the unreal yet familiar place.

It was Rilke or Bachelard who said that the immensity and magnificence of a forest was due to the space between the trees. I hadn't seen anything for more than ten years; almost twenty if you included the world fading into blobs of light and darkness. *In the forest, I am my entire self.* I kept saying it over and over in my head as I walked between the tall trees and tried to understand what was happening to me.

At first, the woods seemed empty. I've always wondered if this was a product of living in the city, where you are numb to the sounds all around you, no matter the time of day. When I could still see I remember visiting a friend's farm that was nestled by a grove of trees. I'd stand on the edge of the grove and look into the woods and feel nothing but emptiness. As I walked, experiencing the space between the trees, I felt that same existential vacancy. At first, anyway. I slowed my pace and tried to pay careful attention to everything around me. The space between the trees felt activated somehow.

Before long there was a break in the trees that gave way to a small clearing. The ground sloped down as I exited the understory. It continued to decline even further down towards a valley.

From the side of the hill I could see the valley jump between hills until it disappeared into a haze. The rough texture of the pines and birches covered all of the rolling hills and was only interrupted by a thin tower of smoke coming from the hill across the valley. With no other place to go, I walked down the hillside to see where the smoke was coming from.

+++

I knew that if I opened my eyes, I would be back in the theater, in a box, seeing it as a flat screen ready for a projection. But eyes closed I was walking around in seemingly endless three-dimensional space.

I'd only experienced something like this one other time in my life. Hana and I once went to an exhibition of James Turrell's new work. Entrance was timed, and we had to put white booties on our shoes. I didn't understand why - the piece we were looking at just looked like a giant blue painting on the wall. It glowed in the most unusual manner, I remember. As I stood looking at the painting, Hana stepped into it.

What I saw as a painting was actually a room lit by blue light. It took all of my mental energy to set aside rationality and try to step through the picture plane into what really was a completely separate room. What seemed flat and static held space. I couldn't help but think of the Turrell piece now, although I wasn't sure how to exit the space in the theater. I'd already tried to step off the stage as I'd come, but any direction I walked was blocked by a wall.

I still don't know which place was more fantastic. Confusion and exhaustion made it difficult to make sense of either situation. I'd heard the wood nymphs only minutes before, sitting next to Jefre and the rest of the audience, and now I was in a stage that wasn't a stage. I must have been sensing some sort of screen that I was able to pass through. Beneath the pine needles and occasional roots, I could still feel the irregularities of the floorboards as I walked in search of any solid objects, and I could sense the technical mechanisms all around the stage. I knew, though, that I was walking into some sort of paradox. Something that would appear flat to anyone in the audience. I moved around the space, trying to find an exit, but things shifted as I walked. My cane would touch a wall that was gone by the time my hands reached it. The only consistent object in the space was a folding chair, which I could feel from time to time, though never where I expected it to be.

Though I had the feeling that this could be hell, another, stronger feeling prevailed: I knew that I did not belong in this paradox. There were many things that I was unsure of in my life, but I can say with absolute certainty that wherever I was, whatever this rectangle that I occupied with my three-dimensional self, I was not supposed to be there. There were things that moved around me, spectral-like presences moving around the edges of my senses, that made sure I understood that I was an unwanted visitor.

I stayed, though, because of the wonder I experienced in the woods. I was hungry for images, and couldn't get enough of the forest. I got glasses when I was four years knew that I would lose my sight entirely before I was forty. In this liminal space, though, I could see again when I closed my eyes.

I continued descending the hillside, to discover the source of the smoke.

+++

I had no idea if the thing on the stage could hurt me while I was in the woods, but it was an easy escape to close my eyes and return to the woods. As I walked down the hillside, I remembered being on the Golden Gate Bridge with Hana, crowded with bodies that I couldn't see. The trees were around me on the hill as I hiked and I could feel their presence around me, pulsing like the people on the bridge even though the trees were tethered to the ground. There were many other people on the bridge that day, and I could only think about the morbid history of the bridge. Without even hesitating, right there in front of all those people, she started to sing to me. Her voice and song always starved the grim thoughts that visited me often. That's one of my most cherished memories with Hana. I hoped for her to sing to me now, to chase away the lingering terror from the stage and whatever was breathing there. The feeling of dread felt sour coursing through my bones and I couldn't shake it, despite the beauty of the forest around me.

It was here that I paused before a switchback and saw a small hut that was the source of the smoke.

Instead of reveling in my situation, the implications and weight of it started to sink in. Could I live here, in this sort of supernatural inner state? Was it temporary? Could I stay? What if there was someone in the house?

+++

Occasionally I stood up from my chair on the stage to confirm that the space was still changing, but otherwise I sat. I felt the specters moving excitedly, still out of reach but affirming the numinous all around. I moved the chair closer to what I determined to be the center of the stage to escape their stirring. I sat for only a moment but felt vulnerable and unprotected. Standing left me feeling more exposed, so I crouched behind the chair and closed my eyes. I could hear someone breathing just over my shoulder.

+++

I stepped through a dry riverbed that cut through the lowest part of the valley. A path ascended up the hill and I made my way up to the hut. The brush changed to trees along the trail. There was mist that snaked through the woods and the house darted in and out of my vision as I walked up.

The hut was clad with rust-colored siding and had windows on all sides. It appeared to be dark inside. Aside from firewood stacked neatly to the side of the house and the smoke coming from the chimney, it was hard to tell if anyone lived there. I stood on the trail near the house for some time before being startled by the owner, who had walked up the hillside without making a sound.

+++

My eyes flew open and I found myself in the flat black rectangle.

"You can call me the director," a voice said.

Holding my eyes closed required a strange form of muscle that I wasn't used to using and I felt a revulsion from shifting from one reality to another abruptly.

"Wait, where am I?" I said. "What happened to the opera?"

"You are in a special part of the theater," she said. "The opera has finished." She paced around the intangible space; I could feel the movements of heavy garments. I couldn't tell her age from her voice, but she smelled of resin, something like charred incense. "I know you—you are familiar to me," she said. "I believe we've met before."

"It seems unlikely," I said. "I'm afraid I don't remember you if we have. Did you direct the opera?" Her words were familiar, but I felt her rigidity, the formality of a school teacher or priest.

"No. Did you enjoy it?"

"I can only remember the very beginning," I said. "With the wood nymphs."

"Ah, yes. *Der Wald* is a very short opera, isn't it."

"I don't remember anything else about it, honestly."

"How did you find yourself in this place?" the director asked.

"I'm not quite certain. I remember the wood nymphs singing and then... feeling, well, strange. And I woke up, I guess, and the theater was empty."

"Perhaps you fainted, or some such."

"Maybe," I said, though I didn't believe that was what had happened. "I think I'm ok, though. I feel fine now."

"Did you come to the opera by yourself? I see that you are blind."

"No, I came with a...with a friend."

"And they left you?"

"Yes, apparently he left. Is it very late?"

"No, not very late," the director said.

"I suppose I should be going, though, if the opera is over."

"You should stay as long as you'd like. I love this theater; I've enjoyed my time here."

"Do you work at this theater?"

"In a manner of speaking, yes. I *volunteer*...I think that would be the most appropriate word."

I felt my own arms around my body, as if I was trying to keep out the cold.

"Again, stay as long as you'd like," she said. "I do not know how easy it will be for you to leave anyway. I'm afraid I can't help you, other than to say everything will be o.k."

She softly touched my shoulder and the space lit up. Something here was very wrong. Vague shapes and a flash of light in a mist of half-visible figures circled in front of me, shoulders hunched, ready to pounce. A weak and translucent partition kept them from me, but I shuddered and looked away. I told myself they were just images and could not get to me, phantom visions caused by stress.

There was something about the affect and voice of the director that reminded me of Dr. Hoffmann, my ophthalmologist. A sickeningly sultry voice and the assurances that everything would be ok, even though she knew it wouldn't be. It wasn't going to be ok. I felt split between these two places and had no idea how to get out of either of them.

The director spoke and the hunched figures vanished. "Do you think you could have fallen asleep?" she asked. "Your eyes were closed when I arrived."

"Maybe. I'm not sure...I don't know what's happening. I can see when I close my eyes."

"Oh really? How profound. Do you see my stage?"

"No. I'm in a forest. A large, sprawling forest. It seems...well I don't know where or when it is. It seems timeless, in some ways."

"Really? That's quite interesting. I lived in a beautiful forest long ago. What are you doing in the woods?"

"I'm standing outside of a small hut."

+++

"Good afternoon," the woman who'd walked up the hillside said.

"Good afternoon." I had no idea what time it was but reciprocated her greeting.

The director and the stage had vanished, and I was back in the forest, by the hut. The woman, coming down the hill towards the house, was carrying sticks in a leather bag behind her back. She had long brown hair pulled to one side and soft eyes. A smaller collecting bag was at her side.

"Are you ok? You seemed to have blacked out there for a minute. Your eyes were closed but you were standing. I thought you might faint."

"I'm ok, thank you. Do you live here?"

"Indeed. I've lived here all of my life," she said proudly. "Would you like to come in for tea?"

"I would enjoy that, thank you."

It wasn't a large home but it was well cared for and comfortable. One whole wall of the house was dedicated to glass jars and drying plants hanging in bunches from a wooden beam that ran above the shelves.

"I'm Nathaniel, by the way," I said.

"Henri. Pleased to meet you."

She put a heavy metal kettle on to a stove burner and opened a cabinet to get two cups. I looked at a bookshelf. It had been so long since I'd read the spines of books. I felt grateful for something that I didn't know I was missing as I read the titles. Many of them were in German and French, neither of which I knew. I noticed a thin volume with the word *Nachtstucke*, which

I recognized from a German composer. Otherwise, I was at a loss for what the bindings said. I reveled in the reading regardless.

There were a handful of titles in English. *Pow Wow or Long-Lost Friends* was one of the strangest, along with a book, which I assumed was a hymnal of sorts, called *Evensong.* I saw a book called *The Preteritions,* and a number of field guides to plants and animals.

"You may look at any of those you wish," Henri said.

I took out a book titled *Arbatel de magia veterum* and handled the first few pages carefully. The smell of the book combined with steeping tea was dream-like. I knew I wouldn't be able to keep my eyes closed much longer, so I sat on a wooden chair and set the book on a table.

+++

All at once I was back on the stage, in that lonely space. I could not see the director but I had a very real sense that she would linger in the space, too, and I found no comfort in it. The things I saw when she touched me were even harder to explain than regaining my sight with closed eyes or being in the woods. My shoulders hunched and body tensed in the paradox, as if it would protect me from the director.

I sat back down in the folding chair, not wanting to leave, for risk it would take me out of the woods. I heard thick static as I sat in the strange space and, through it, Hana singing.

She sang in a language that I didn't know and couldn't place. It sounded exactly like the wood nymph at the beginning of the opera, singing about the briefness and ephemerality of life, but I knew it was Hana.

It was fitting, I guess, for Hana to visit me here, in this strange place. Our relationship had always been unorthodox. Our first date was literally going to the Department of Motor Vehicles so she could get a license. She hadn't ever driven and wanted desperately to own her own car.

Her song continued, and I wondered what would happen if I fell asleep. I wanted to fall asleep, but I also wanted to return to Henri's cabin.

+++

"You ok?" Henri asked. I guessed her to be about thirty years old, but I felt a wisdom around her movements and words. Without her bundle of sticks, she moved lightly around her home.

"Yeah, sorry. Did I black out again?"

"I think so. Your eyes were closed but I could see them moving under your lids. You were muttering something, but I couldn't understand it. I tried to shake you. Drink some tea, it might help."

"What kind of tea is it?"

"A blend, from the woods. It's got wild raspberry leaf, lemon balm, fir needles, and a few other herbs in it. It's very good at calming one's nerves."

"It's lovely, thank you."

"Where are you headed?" Henri asked.

"I don't know, actually."

"Well take care at night, it's not the best place to be alone."

"Are there others that live near here?"

"There is a small town not too far from here, but otherwise we're about a half day's walk to the next city. I deliver wood to the town most days."

"Is there a place I might stay in the town?"

"I can give you a name. She'll gladly let you lodge as you need."

"Thank you very much. You're a woodcutter, then?"

"It's one of the things I am. The townspeople don't often come to the woods anymore, so they rely on me to bring them wood for their fireplaces."

"Is something wrong with these woods?"

"No more than any other woods."

"Why don't they come here, then? It seems far too beautiful to ignore without reason."

"There are stories, I suppose. Of a person, a hunter. Someone who patrols the woods."

"Patrols?"

"Yes. I'm not sure how to state it another way. Some of the people from town say he has a pack of hunting dogs. He's a collector, I guess."

"Have you seen this hunter?"

"Gorym. That's what they say his name is. And no, I haven't seen him or his dogs."

I traced the top of my teacup thinking about what Henri said. She picked up the book I had looked at and carefully turned some of the pages.

"You know, this is an interesting book," she said. "Some people say that it is the white wizard's guide. Others say that it is the closest thing to a Christian book of magic."

"And what do you think?"

"I think it is more along the lines of everyday magic. Like the *Pow Wow* book over there. Magic for common folk, which isn't really magic."

"What do you mean?"

"If it is to help you live, it's not really magic. Magic is a designation by someone outside of the reality of the thing that is magical."

"Everyday magic. That's interesting. Can I ask you something else?"

"Sure, please."

"I was attending an opera. In a big city. With a friend. And the opera started, and I watched it, and something happened. You see...I'm blind. I must have passed out during the opera or something. When I woke up, I was alone in the theater. I walked up onto the stage but—as strange as this will sound—the space of the stage was gone, and it was a flat square. Like a blank black screen. Somehow I was in it, somehow I'm *still* in it. When I close my eyes here, they're open in that flat black rectangle. When I open them here, they're closed in that rectangle. I can see here, though, when my eyes are closed there. I'm sure I'm not making any sense at all."

"It is indeed a strange situation," said Henri. "What, though, is your question?"

+++

I jolted awake. I must have fallen asleep; apparently my head falling forward woke me. Sleep was as it had always been—

solitary, neither the woods nor the screen. I was in some vague place without atmosphere, vignettes of different lives coming and going as they pleased.

I had dreamt about Dr. Hoffmann, my childhood ophthalmologist. She was examining my eyes through that big machine and telling me that everything was going to be ok. I saw shapes that didn't make sense; low, four-legged things running towards me in the little lenses as Dr. Hoffmann adjusted the lenses with a clack. She could tell I was nervous and said that she was right there and that everything would be ok. She put her hand on my leg, waking me up.

I could still hear thick layers of static and Hana singing. It was as if her voice had been recorded on an ancient record player. The distortion somehow made her voice even more beautiful.

I got off of the chair onstage and lay down. It wasn't the hard wood of a typical theater stage, however. It felt soft, almost like well-maintained grass, but it had no smell to it. I rested my head on my hands and listened to Hana singing in some strange language and drifted to sleep again, hopefully to return once more to the phantasmagoric wood.

The singing in the paradox and noise of the woods mixed in some sort of bizarre meshing of my new reality. I knew that Hana was somewhere in these worlds that shouldn't exist. Whether it was a haunted theater or some fault in my own mind, I had no idea.

I held out hope, though, that this strangeness might lead me to Hana.

Three

I opened my eyes to see Henri standing over me.

"I was worried you'd faint, so I moved you to my bed."

"Thank you," I said, slowly getting up. "I think I'm fine, though. Thanks much for the tea."

"My pleasure. I packed some things for you to take with you."

She handed me a basket with a vibrant blue tea blend and some crackers and an apple.

"Thank you, I really don't know what to say. This is too kind."

"Not at all. I'm happy to help. Keep along that path and you'll reach town before the sun sets."

I walked toward the front door and, instead of saying thanks again, I smiled and nodded out of reverence. The young wood-cutter was really unlike anyone I'd ever met.

The trail continued uphill a bit further until it rounded the hill. It was relatively level for the rest of the walk. The air had gotten colder and I pulled my coat closer around to keep the chill out. The trees, standing close enough that I was sure their branches were tangled in the overstory, blocked any wind but also blocked the sun, preventing its warmth from reaching the earth.

I don't know how long I'd walked when I saw the dogs. I stopped in my tracks, worried that I'd somehow stumbled upon a place I wasn't supposed to be. Thoughts of what Henri had said about the townspeople and not being in the woods after dark sparked my anxiety. I somehow knew, though, that the dogs wouldn't hurt me. A deep knowledge that overrode all of the fear that I had.

I started walking slowly towards the dogs sitting along the trail. I could hear strange melodies through the trees; songs sung in different languages, even though I was sure that I was the only person around.

"Hello, pups," I said as they sat, tongues out, watching me walk toward them. They were massive animals and looked like a mix of wolf and mastiff.

They stood panting, waiting for me to speak.

"Would you like to take a walk with me?" I didn't know what else to say.

With that, the two dogs stood and turned to walk with me along the trail. We walked, one dog on either side of me, for a couple hundred yards when I heard a great barking coming from the woods and watched a third dog fall in line behind us. The four of us, then, continued on the trail.

+++

The trees thinned out and I could see the town. The trail led along the side of a hill to a gate on the edge of town. The fence was modest but seemed sturdy enough to keep out the things of the woods the townspeople were afraid of.

The dogs followed me to the gate but lay down along the wooden fence and would go no further. I glanced at them once more and they looked at me forlornly and then looked away. I tore off pieces of bread and gave it to the dogs before leaving them.

I had the strangest sensation as I walked through the gate. I couldn't tell if it was some sort of goose flesh or I'd unknowingly walked through a swarm of small insects, but I felt things crawling all over me, as if my nerves were sending small electrical shocks all over my body and tiny legs scurried amidst the hairs on my arms and legs.

"Hello," a strong voice said. I looked around for a guard, or someone near the gate, but it was a small man with a goat on a leash. He looked to be walking out, and I was intimidated by him, despite his stature.

"Hello," I said. "I'm passing through the woods and I wondered if I might find a place to stay for the night."

"Surely yes, the pub has rooms for let. You'll see the sign just down the Main Street."

"Thank you much."

His face held the same expression during our quick exchange, stern and suspicious of me as a visitor. "I wouldn't go back out to the woods after dark, just to be safe."

"I won't," I said. "I met Henri the woodcutter and she gave me the same warning."

"Very well. Have a good evening."

I looked back at the gate and saw that the dogs were still waiting outside, watching my movements. They did not even attempt to come in. I suspected that they'd disappear when I turned my back, searching for someone else, perhaps someone who would share their food.

Music played through the town; it sounded like an aria from the opera, but slower and quieter, as if muffled by the thick walls of a house. It was a part of the aria that the singer who had a voice just like Hana had sung, this time, though, at a snail's pace. I couldn't be sure, but it seemed as though parts of the paradox were bleeding through to this town in the woods, or vice versa.

I did not get a sense of welcome from the people I passed. Most walked with purpose, so perhaps I was just not a part of their daily routines, but the few children I saw hid in the alleyways instead of acknowledging my presence.

The village was mostly quaint little houses, with a few shops along the Main Street as well. There was one building that was taller than the rest, but it appeared to be shuttered, and there were brightly painted wooden circles on all of the windows. The paintings stuck out; the rest of the buildings were made of sandy and neutral colors, aside from the vegetable and flower gardens attached to a number of the houses, but the paintings on this building were bright and eccentric. They had dizzying patterns and symbols of fire and other elements. I could not even imagine what the paintings were for, looking out above all of the other buildings in the town.

I found the pub - *The Owl and Eye,* according to the sign - and entered. Aside from two people behind the bar, it was empty. I ordered a beer and set the basket down at a table near a fireplace. I didn't know where I was exactly, but the bar was very much an English country pub, with a great old hearth and dark wood matching the yellow stone buildings throughout the town. It felt like a storybook.

The server set my beer on a napkin and walked away, leaving me alone to drink. Though I knew I was experiencing this in every real sense of the word, there was something fuzzy at the edges that I couldn't put my finger on. The beer was refreshing, and I tried to enjoy what was happening. I tried very hard.

A young woman came and tended the fire in the fireplace.

"It's a beautiful fireplace," I said.

"Thank you. It is quite old, as you can see." She didn't look at me when she spoke but kept to her task, adding another log and straightening the cord stacked to the left of the fireplace.

"Someone told me there might be a room to rent for the night here."

"We do have rooms," she said. "Would you like to take one for the night? I'm sure you are tired from traveling."

"I would like one, please. Do you serve food? I think I'd like to take something up to my room if that's possible."

"Of course, sir. I'll get your room straightened out and bring a menu. Someone will bring it upstairs."

"Thank you. Could I bother you with one more question?"

"Of course."

"When I was walking down the Main Street, I heard singing, but it sounded far away. Do you know where it might have been coming from?"

"You can sometimes hear singing from the woods. I'm not sure that is what you heard, but the sound can carry from the trees behind the houses on West Street. I think most folks here think it is a bad omen."

"Why is that?"

"Well, it's a bit embarrassing, really; I'm not one for superstition even though most folks around here are. A lot of people say that the singing comes from hamadryads in the forest."

"I don't even know what that is."

"It's...well, it's a sort of spirit figure that is bonded to a tree. A nymph, I suppose. Just much, much larger. They supposedly protect the trees in the forest. My grandmother always said it was the tree in and of itself, that the trees were singing to prove how brief our lives are. They sing all of the time, she used to say, but we can only hear them when our time has been limited somehow."

"Limited? That's quite interesting."

"Limited in the sense that a decision we've made or an emotion we've felt that seems to be particularly burdensome is really just a single moment in the life of the trees, or of the hamadryads. My grandmother said that the hamadryads thought they were immortal, but they really just live a very long time. I think it was just a way for gran to tell me to cheer up. That any bad feelings didn't matter in the end, because they were so fleeting."

"Well, that answers my question, I guess."

"Yes sir. And one last thing—we're supposed to tell all visitors that they shouldn't leave the town at night. There are lights in the village, but please do not leave beyond the gate until morning."

"Because of the hunter?"

"The hunter, yes, but also the great number of bears and wolves in the woods, among other things. We love living near the forest, but it really is an untamed place."

"So I've heard, from Henri and others."

"Ah, so you've met Henri. She's quite nice. Most folks here treat her as a superstition as well."

"Really? She seems perfectly normal to me."

"It's hard, sometimes, for people who think they are normal to understand why someone would want to live alone, without a family, out in the woods."

"Do they think she's a witch?"

"Some probably do, though they rely on her for firewood because they are too scared to fetch it themselves."

"Do you think she's a witch?"

"I think she marches to the beat of her own drummer, as they say. This small town has a lot of nice things to offer, but they all come at a price. I'll get your room sorted and bring you a menu for dinner."

As she walked away, I saw it in her gait and the way she held her shoulders: she reminded me greatly of my Hana.

+++

I had trouble sleeping in the room above the pub, in part because it was a new place, but also because I was afraid of returning to the anomalous empty black screen when I closed my eyes. I wasn't sure it would happen - and the times my eyelids became so heavy I couldn't keep my eyes open, I hadn't returned to that space, but rather to some bizarre quasi-dream state that presented many figures, all with comic proportions, and some with antlers or other shamanic features that presented as a sort of council for my current state of living in two different worlds. I felt like I didn't belong and that the people in my waking dream (as I would not allow myself to sleep fully) were judging me. My eyes would open and see the now familiar surroundings of the simple room above the pub and, when the weight of them was too great, they'd close and the council would scorn me with their eyes.

I moved a chair close to the window and sat up, looking out the window. I could see the Main Street of the town from my room. Lanterns still had a soft glow to them, breaking up the blue darkness into a somewhat regular grid. I could see clearly where the town ended, and I could see that a tall fence surrounded all sides of the town.

The wood was dark and dense. My room for the night was on the third floor and looked into the top quarters of the pine and birch. I could see the contours of some of the trees by the glow of the streetlamps, but otherwise, the wood was dark.

Toward the base of the trees, I could see eyes reflecting the light, the type of ghost eyes that are made for hunting at night. They moved as if standing guard outside the fence of the town; sometimes reflecting green and other times reflecting red.

I saw something else in the window, too; I strained to see it completely because I couldn't quite make out my disembodied reflection; I looked horrible, grizzled. I had no idea where I'd gotten these clothes. When I stood up from my seat I noticed that my face was filled with anger. I didn't feel the hate that I wore on my face. It had been so long since I'd seen my own reflection and it was quite a shock.

I moved my hand up to my face and the reflection stood still; its arms didn't move. I moved my other hand, waving it to disprove the apparition as a trick of the light, and what I thought was the reflection in the window stood still and cracked a wide smile. The reflection had sharpened teeth, decayed and stained. I backed away from the window and nearly tripped over the bed but the reflection stood its ground, hovering in the window.

It was clear that the one that haunted the woods made himself visible in my window, a floating specter amidst the darkness of the trees. *The Huntsman,* I said to the empty room. The reflection smiled again and I exited the room, forgetting to grab my key before the door latched shut. I thought that, perhaps, I could hear the hamadryads singing because my time was limited in another sense.

+++

I could hear soft music coming from downstairs so I walked quietly down to see if I could be let into my room. My footsteps sounded like thunder in the quiet building and I hoped I didn't wake anyone else up.

The music was from a man playing the zither at one of the tables in the pub. The bar was otherwise empty, and the last of the fire cracked as the man played the stringed instrument quietly. He said his name was Victor and he managed the pubs most nights. I would have guessed him a poet or a philosopher if I met him on the street; his eyes were the color of slate and his hair and beard unkempt, but his whole presence felt light, perhaps because of his music.

"Sorry to interrupt, but I've locked myself out of my room."

"Oh no problem, I can have someone let you back in," he said. "Can I get you a drink while you are down here? You look as though you could use one."

"I could do with a nightcap," I said, and I realized that his voice reminded me of Jefre's.

"It's almost sunrise, so I think we're a bit past being able to call it a nightcap," he said. "I can mix it with some coffee, unless you were hoping for some sleep."

"I think I'm past the hope of sleep."

"Very well, coffee plus coming right up."

"Thank you."

"Where are you from?"

"I'm not exactly sure how to explain it," I said.

"Try me. I know lots of places, even those that aren't well known."

"I'm from the city, I guess."

"Ah, that's a pretty well-known place."

"I went to an opera in an old theater and, somehow, ended up walking in the woods. You sound a lot like my friend that I went to the opera with, strangely."

"Ah. I love the opera. Which one did you see?"

"*Der Wald*. Though I didn't see much of it."

"I've not heard of that one. What do you mean you didn't see it?"

"I remember hearing an aria, but not much else. I woke up in an empty theater, walked onto the stage, and I was here. Or, not here, actually, in the woods."

"The woods will do that to you, for sure. And don't get me started on nymphs."

I laughed. Even amidst everything that'd happened, his statement still sounded preposterous.

"This is a bit of a strange place, really," he went on. "I've lived here all of my life, so I'm used to it, I guess. Everyone is afraid of the woods. Everyone is sort of afraid of the person that brings us our firewood, but we rely on her for it. And everyone is full of superstition."

"Henri?"

"Ah, yes. So you met the witch of the wood?"

"Yes," I laughed. "She didn't seem much like a witch to me."

"She's not. But superstition sees all sorts of things. Like you, you look a bit like the pictures of the huntsman everyone is so afraid of."

"Really?"

"Yes. Same face, same build. You don't have any of the weapons the huntsman is supposed to have, though. Unless they're in your room, of course." He gave a wry smile.

"I don't make it a habit of carrying weapons," I said.

"Ah, there you have it!"

I was enjoying this friendly banter with Victor. For a moment, things felt almost normal.

"Try not to take offense if the people around here don't take a liking to you, though," he went on. "It's because they've been taught from a very young age to fear the woods. A lot of that fear comes from the hunter."

"I don't think I'll be here much longer, honestly. I've enjoyed my time, but I'm not sure I'll be able to stay."

"Did you come from the direction of Henri's house?"

I nodded.

"You should go the other direction," he said. "The woods are even more beautiful to the east. There are a few lookout points I'd highly recommend."

"I thought you didn't leave town?"

"I don't, officially. But I may have seen a few things." He grinned again. "I can loan you a horse, if you can promise to come back this direction before you leave. Do you ride?"

"It's been a while," I said. Actually I couldn't remember the last time I'd ridden a horse. And even that was a miniature pony when I was very young.

"Don't worry, it won't be a problem," he said. "I'm finished working at 7—want to meet me downstairs after you've eaten breakfast?"

"Sure, thanks."

+++

Another couple made their way in shortly after Victor left. I ate breakfast in silence while they talked about their plans for the day. When I was done, Victor met me near the bar and led me to the stables.

"This is Hesperides," Victor said, brushing the dark gray horse's hair. "She's a good horse."

"I can't thank you enough," I said. "I'll return before sunset and put her back in her stall, if that's ok."

"That works well for me, enjoy your ride."

Victor waved as I rode off on Hesperides. I was surprised at how easy the horse was to ride. I struggled a bit at first, but Hesperides was responsive and patient. I felt a strong bond with her even before we reached the forest.

We got to the eastern gate of the village and four dogs waited just outside. Three were the dogs from the night before and the new one looked similar, but were even larger and mostly black, slightly darker than Hesperides' own coat.

"Good morning," I said to the dogs.

A woman carrying a bundle of sticks leered at me as I approached the gate.

"Those beasts are foul," the woman said. Her back was bent carrying the sticks and she shuffled slowly across the street. Hesperides and I stopped to let her pass. "I'd stay out of those woods if you know what is good for you."

"Have a pleasant day," I said, not wanting to engage with her negativity.

She started singing as she finished crossing the street and Hesperides and I continued through the gate. It was a deep mournful chant, sung in rhythm with the horse's gait, and quite mesmerizing. It ended abruptly, and I felt myself being lulled into some deeper state of discomfort.

I crossed the short distance between the town's gate and the trail into the woods with the four dogs following behind. Victor had given me a hand-drawn map and I headed towards an overlook.

The woods seemed lighter, not as dense on this side of the village. The ride was meditative with the cadence of the horse and the dogs running ahead, waiting, and smelling everything they could. It lulled me into a near-transcendent state such that, when I saw her, I didn't believe my eyes.

But it was her, it was Hana.

She was standing in the trail, smiling. The woods around her, already airy, burst into bright light and sparks of joy. The last twenty years of my life had been spent missing her, wondering why she had gone or if she was still alive, and there she was, standing on the trail, waiting for me.

Everything and nothing made sense; I still didn't know where I was or how long I'd be able to stay, or if I was even really alive. Hana was here, though, and that was all I needed. I would do everything in my power to stay here, no matter the cost.

Four

I awoke, suddenly, and smelled the dry plywood and musty stage of the theater. I could feel someone, or something, nearby.

"Hello?" I said.

"Hello again," the director said. "How are you? You must be enjoying yourself, if you've spent all this time here."

"I am. I'm not quite sure what's happening, but I am enjoying myself. May I stay? I'd like to close my eyes again and—"

"You may stay, but I must insist that we speak before you sleep again. The things that are happening are using a great deal of energy, including your own. You must, how should I say it...*earn* that energy, or pay compensation for it."

"Anything, I'll give you anything. Just tell me, please... I just saw someone that I've been looking for for a very long time. Was that...real?"

"Ah, yes. That is something that happens quite often in the woods." I could hear soft footsteps and felt the pressure of the screen and stage change. "I will devise a list of possible, well, payments, but perhaps we can start off by you supplying the name of the nice fellow who brought you to the opera. He was taller and, if you don't mind me saying, handsomer than you. I would very much like to get to know him."

"Jefre? Is he here? Did you see him?"

"In a manner of speaking, yes. What is his last name?"

"Jefre Corbin."

"Very good. Thank you."

"Why would you like to meet him?"

"Does it matter? It gives you more time in the woods, with her. It is a her, yes?"

"Yes, but the woods aren't real, are they?"

"Oh indeed, they are very real. Real in the sense that I wouldn't do anything dangerous in there."

"What do you mean?"

"If you were to fall off your horse in the woods, for example, you would be 'really' hurt. You might not make it back here. Or if you were to run into something monstrous."

I shifted on the ground and realized that I was still lying down. I felt as though I was standing up, conversing with the director, but no, there I was on the ground. I got the sense that she was floating above me, parallel, talking to me as if we were standing up.

"What is this space?" I said. "Nothing makes sense here. Where am I?"

"Don't you remember? You came to the theater, and you walked up on stage."

"Yes, but...something isn't right. This space...this isn't really the stage, is it."

"For all purposes, yes, it is the stage. But it is something more, too, you could say."

"A screen?"

"Not a screen, though it might look like that if you could see it. It is a non-place."

"A non-place!"

"Yes. To most, it doesn't exist. Yet it is a place that you and I and a few select beings can inhabit. A non-place."

"I don't understand at all."

"Nor do I expect you to. Yet. But for now, I know something else you could provide for me, something that would allow your journeys in the woods to continue."

"What is it? Please, I'll do anything to return."

"I need to speak with Victor."

"Victor? From the pub?"

"Yes. I need to speak with him urgently. If you could bring him out to the woods, it will be a great help to me."

"Does he know you?"

"I believe he does. I am the director. You needn't tell him about me, though, just bring him to the woods."

I wasn't at all certain about her intentions, and she saw my hesitation.

"If you choose not to fulfill my request," she said, "you'll remain here, with nothing but the specters that occupy the Screen. I cannot promise that you'd ever be able to return."

"So it *is* a screen."

"It is to most people. In any case it's the easiest thing to call this place...the no-place you find yourself. You can just stay here."

The director walked around, heavy shoes clicking loudly on the floor. I waited for more explanation, but she was silent. Finally I couldn't take it anymore.

"O.k.," I said, "I'll bring Victor out to the woods. Then I can stay there forever, with Hana?"

"No, not forever. Nothing is forever. But you may stay here for longer, yes."

"What about the things on the other side of the Screen? Can they get through?"

"I will keep you safe from them," she said in a saccharine voice.

I had to see Hana again and be with her, be in the same place as her. I told the director I would bring Victor out into the woods before sundown, ignoring any qualms I had about the reckoning that could follow.

Five

When I closed my eyes again, it was no longer Hana in the woods, but Henri, gathering sticks in a large bundle on her back. She walked down the trail purposefully and stopped when she saw Hesperides and me approaching.

"Hello, that's a fine horse you found," she said. "And some dogs. If I were superstitious, I'd say you looked like—well, never mind."

"Hello," I said and patted the horse on his neck. "Victor in the village lent him to me, so I could explore the woods a bit more. Did you see anyone else out here?"

"I haven't seen anyone since I dropped firewood off in town yesterday. Did you?"

"Yes, or at least I thought I did. Someone I used to know but haven't seen in a long time."

"Really? Are you sure it wasn't me?"

"No...it wasn't you, it was...I had to open my eyes for a few minutes, I guess I'm not sure how much time passed while I was away."

"Did you have your eyes closed while you were riding? You're putting a lot of trust in that horse you just met."

"No, it's difficult to explain. I...I'm somewhere else, too. I was in an old theater and I walked up onto the stage and, when I closed my eyes, I ended up here."

"So you're dreaming, then." Henri shifted her weight, and the bundle of sticks on her back moved slightly.

"I don't think so. Someone is talking to me there, though. I'm really confused by all of it, I'm not sure what's real and what isn't. I just want to see Hana." I felt my own hand rubbing my temples instinctively.

"Is it Hana you thought you saw in the woods?"

"Yes. We were married long ago, and then she left."

"Oh, I'm sorry to hear," Henri said. She set her bag of sticks down on the ground and looked more comfortable. "There's an old theater in town, too, you know. Victor might have told you about it. It's really quite beautiful."

"No, he didn't. Are you heading there with those sticks?"

"I am. I usually bring kindling in the morning and firewood in the afternoon. You know, if you need to talk to someone, you can always come back to the cabin. I'm not much of a people person, but your problem is an interesting one, for sure."

"Thank you. Victor gave me some places I should see before I leave. I'd better let you to your work."

"Sure, take care. Maybe I'll see you again sometime, to talk about your problem."

"I'd like that very much," I said. Henri stepped off the path and the dogs and I continued, walking through the trees that stood like statues.

+++

The overlook that Victor had pointed me to was quite the spectacle. I was distracted, thinking about ways to bring Victor to the woods, but I was still able to observe the exalted splendor of the forest all of the way up to that small rock outcropping that looked down into the rolling hills below. The hills looked like sleeping monsters that would shift and change the landscape if I closed my eyes again.

My plan was simple: I was going to tie Hesperides up in the forest and tell Victor that something was wrong with her and ask him to come out and take a look. It was still the middle of the afternoon, but the sun was setting by the time I could see the fence around the village through the trees. It was cool in the woods. I made my way back through the gate and found Victor, waiting by the horse's stall.

I looked at my hands and they were still. Before, anything like this would have sent me into nervousness and my hands would shake. Now I was calm, and as I walked up to him, I could feel my heartbeat in my ears, its regular and even slowed beating providing my cadence.

"Where's the horse?" Victor said. "Did you have a good ride?"

"I did indeed, but I think there might be something wrong with her," I said. "She's tied up to a tree just inside the woods, could you come take a look?"

"Sure, but we have to hurry, the gate will be closing soon."

"O.k." He ran to me before I could get any closer, and we turned back towards the forest.

The dogs, as usual, were waiting just outside the gate.

"What are they doing here?" Victor asked.

"They started following me when I entered the woods. The two smaller right after I left Henri's house, and the larger ones when I started out with your horse today."

"I can't say I'm happy to see them," he said. "They don't seem friendly."

"I haven't had much problem with them. They waited outside the gate overnight for me to leave the village."

Victor's reaction to that was one I couldn't read; it looked dismissive, but also slightly concerned.

"Okay so where is the horse?" he said. "What seemed to be wrong with her?"

"She was limping, favoring one leg. I was quite concerned. She's just over here," I said and walked further down the trail.

That's when I saw her. The director was wrapped in a dark purple cloak over heavy gray woolen clothes, and petting Hesperides.

Victor started walking quickly toward the horse. "Who is she?" he called over his shoulder.

I told him I didn't know, which was only partially true. Victor ran up ahead of me, and when I caught up to him he was talking to her.

"Can I take my horse back, please," he said. "The village gates are closing soon and I need to get her back to her stall before dark." Victor's voice strived for politeness, but came across as panicked and worried.

"I think his leg is injured," the director said. Her eyes were dark against her pale skin. They held my gaze so much that I tripped over the root of a tree that emerged from the uneven path. I could see a trail of blood running down the horse's leg that hadn't been there before.

"I think we'll be able to make it, I'll lead her in and not ride her," Victor said.

He got close enough to untie the bridle when the director opened her arms, as if to give Victor a hug. But a dark light emitted from her chest and Victor gasped. His hand dropped from the bridle and he began to walk toward the director, accepting her macabre embrace, the black light changing the color of his skin. As he drew closer his body began to evaporate and melt, leaving nothing but an after-image of Victor floating in the air.

I stopped, still twenty feet away, horrified. "What the hell happened to him!" I said.

The director turned to me and put her finger to her lips. Her face reminded me of Dr. Hoffmann, one of the few faces that has lingered in my mind since I lost my vision. I fell to my knees on the trail. The trees were spinning and the dogs moved through the woods and positioned themselves around me. I gave in to the weight of the day and the horror of what I'd just witnessed and collapsed onto the trail. I saw the director's feet and dress as she walked away. My eyes closed from some combination of exhaustion and terror and misery, only to open in the world I now knew as the Screen.

Six

"You didn't have to come back, you could have stayed longer," the director said.

Her voice faded in and out, circling around my head. I didn't know what to say. I sat on the chair and hung my head. I didn't close my eyes for fear that I'd be back in the woods. Every word from the director put me on edge.

"I'll be leaving now," I said, with as much anger and forcefulness as I could gather.

"But I just got here," a new but familiar voice said.

Jefre! I had led my friend right into this nightmare. "Jefre," I said. "You have to get out of here!" I said "This place is—"

I felt his arms around my shoulders. "Hush now," he said. "You're just having one of your weird visions. It will pass soon, like all the others."

I couldn't tell for sure, but it felt like Jefre and the director were smiling at each other.

I lowered my voice, hoping only Jefre could hear me. "We need to leave," I said. "Jefre, help me get out."

Jefre took my arm and we walked to where I'd come up the steps, but there was nothing there. The edge felt like hard and cold glass, and I couldn't find an opening.

"Can you see a way to get out?" I said.

I could hear the director singing a soft melody as I stood with Jefre. I recognized it as the song that lulled me into some sort of trance from the opera, slightly lower than Hana's own voice. I could hear screeches that seemed to be coming from above, distant and high. Jefre was preternaturally calm, which made me feel frenetic and unsure what was happening.

"Please, Jefre, you have to tell me where I am. What is this place?"

"It's not really a place," he said. "It's four walls, but they are...not fixed, you could say. Right now they're made of wood and metal, but they've changed since I came here."

"How did you get here?"

"You asked me to meet you here, remember? The opera isn't until tomorrow night, though. I saw you on the stage..."

"Have you talked to the director?"

"Who? There was no one else in the theater. I called your name when I saw you, but you couldn't hear me. You looked like you were sleeping." I felt his feet shift as we talked and the slick sound of dress shoes on the plywood stage.

"Do you hear the singing?"

"No. I can't hear anything, it's quiet here."

"I hear music and something above us, too. Screeches, moving around quickly above us."

Rats in the woodwork, my stepfather used to say.

"There's nothing up there," he said. "The ceiling is very high, though, so I suppose you could be hearing something. I can't see the rafters or the top, it's too dark."

"Can you just take me home? I'm done with this...I saw her, though. I saw Hana."

"You saw who?"

"Hana."

I could hear Jefre's impatience, and I could hear him scratching his thumb with his index finger; something he always did when he was frustrated, hands balled in a fist.

"Look, I've tried to be patient about this, Nathaniel. You didn't see Hana. You've just idealized her. I'm so sorry that all this happened to you, but you just have to let go."

"I saw her in the woods."

"What woods? The set, to the opera?"

"No. Somewhere else. I can see the woods when I close my eyes."

"This isn't making sense."

"I know. And I'm telling you, there's someone here. Right now. She spoke to me just before you told me you were here."

"Hana?"

"No. I saw Hana in the woods. The *director* is here. She's still here, somewhere, I can feel—"

"Hello. You must be Jefre," the director said. "Pleased to meet you."

+++

Jefre was startled and he gave a nervous laugh.

"Hi, nice to meet you too," he said. "I was hoping to take my friend home, could you tell us where the exit is?"

"Of course. The easiest exit would be through the back doors. Would you like to join me for some tea, first?"

"No thank you, my friend isn't well and we should get going."

Jefre helped me over to the door and I heard him turn the handle.

"It's locked," he said.

"Oh, my. Well, that is unfortunate," said the director. "I suppose we'll have to wait until the security guard makes his rounds. He should be by shortly."

Jefre led me back to the metal chair and I realized there were now two, next to each other, where there had been only one. The quiet squeaks and chirps high above us continued. I leaned close to Jefre, doing my best to whisper in his ear. "Do you see her? What does she look like?"

Before he could answer I felt her force her way between Jefre and me, pushing us aside with great force. I fell off the chair and heard a series of quick staccato clicks, as if Jefre or the director was clenching their jaws over and over again rapidly. Jefre screamed. I got up and reached out to push the director away, but there was nothing to push, and I touched the side of Jefre's face, feeling his beard.

Jefre screamed again. I felt something hot and wet on his face as the chittering of teeth continued.

"Something's biting me!" Jefre yelled. "Get it off me!"

I felt around madly for anything I could grab but I could only find Jefre, squirming and writhing in the chair until he fell to the floor. I covered him with my body, hoping to protect him from whatever was attacking him, but all I could feel was empty space. All the while something, some specter, maybe, continued to gnaw at him.

Jefre's screams turned to sobs, and eventually those diminished. I thought he was dead; I touched his body and moved him, but he lay still. I gently put my hand on his rib cage and felt it rise and fall.

"I know you're here!" I cried to the director. "What did you do to him?"

There was no answer, only movement, like great wings or flowing robes.

"What do you want?" I screamed into the torrent.

I felt it, then, the hot, sick, blunt teeth gnawing at me. I tried to push away whatever was biting me but there was nothing there. My hands flailed at empty space. The pain was incredible; I could feel blood running down the back of my neck and into my shirt, and I screamed. I fell to the floor and curled up. The gnawing didn't stop until I passed out.

Seven

In the woods, it was as if I hadn't left. I was collapsed on the trail, looking at strange viscera that I assumed to be what was left of Victor. The director was nowhere to be found. Hesperides stood as if nothing had happened, and the dogs waited for my command.

My hands were shaking uncontrollably and the woods were surreal; I felt surrounded by witnesses that never materialized. I inspected the blood on the horse's leg and saw no visible cuts. As evening was quickly turning to night and she appeared to be fine, I mounted Hesperides and kicked her to a gallop toward the gate. I had no interest in spending the night out in the woods, nor going back to the Screen.

As we rode I heard bells from somewhere in the village. I was hopeful that it didn't signal the closing of the gates.

We arrived to find the gate closed and fortified. I got off Hesperides and checked the gate, but it wouldn't budge. I stood next to the horse - my horse, now, I supposed - in the growing darkness.

I wept outside the gate. Guilt, fear, and that dark well of dread deep inside all joined in a torrent of emotions. I kneeled and covered my face as I wept. There must be some way to forge ahead, I thought, staying true to my goal of finding Hana. But at what cost? Look what had happened to Victor and Jefre. Everything inside me was conflicted, thoughts and feelings engaged in full hostility towards one another.

I picked myself up and wiped my face. I mounted Hesperides and continued west, towards the only other place I knew in these woods.

+++

Before long, I saw a figure that I assumed was Henri, carrying a bag for hiking. I called and the figure turned around; I saw Henri's wiry hair as she waved.

"Hello," she said, as we approached.

"Good to see you, Henri. I'm afraid I've gotten locked out of the village."

"Ah, yes. They can't be too careful. Their stars always spell disaster, if you know what I mean."

I smiled even though I didn't fully understand.

"You're more than welcome to follow me if you'd like," she said. "We can figure out a place for you to sleep."

"That's very kind of you, thanks."

"I'm glad you met Victor, he's a great person. One of my favorites in town, for sure."

"Yeah, he is very kind as well," I said. I don't know why I said it, but my blood was sour with guilt and I couldn't stand still. My eyes looked just over Henri's shoulder, not wanting to make eye contact, as I would have surely confessed to what had happened.

"Victor understands, well, you know...my situation."

"That you'd rather live alone?"

"Yes, that's about the sum of it."

I could feel Henri confiding in me, and I looked back at her face and made eye contact. "I've been alone for far too long," she said. "It can make one...strange."

"Yes, I suppose it could," I said, absently.

"I was thinking about that old theater some more, while I was collecting wood today," Henri said. "It is quite a remarkable story. To think that they believe the greatest danger to them is out in the woods..."

Now she had my full attention. "What do you mean?"

"Well, their whole lives revolve around staying out of the woods. I bring them wood, and small animals. There are a handful of foragers and hunters that travel outside of the village, but generally, it's seen as bad luck to leave the village unless absolutely required. People get shunned for walking into the woods."

"Really. How do they get food, then?"

"They grow most of their own food. They raise livestock in the back corner of the village for meat, and most everyone has their own garden." Hesperides had slowed down to match Henri's pace. The dogs were nowhere to be seen; I assumed they must have run off or ran ahead. I had started growing fond of the feral animals.

"What about the theater?"

"Ah, yes, the old theater. I've only ever heard stories, but they are...more detailed, perhaps, than the ones I've heard about the huntsman. It's not used anymore, but the building still stands near the center of the village."

I wondered what Henri would say if she knew about Victor. I could still hear the blunt teeth that attacked Jefre, too, as my two worlds bled into one another. There was a fog on this side of the woods and I could smell crushed pineapple weed under the horse's footsteps. I felt some safety with Henri, but also felt on the verge of collapse, from sheer emotional exhaustion. Making matters worse, anger was rising within me, an anger I didn't understand and that I struggled to contain.

"The theater was always considered a village theater of sorts," Henri continued, "where locals interested in acting could perform for the other people in town. Musicians played there as well; it was a gathering place, or at least it once was."

I listened intently, Henri's story punctuated by Hesperides hooves and the gentle sound of fabric on fabric with Henri's backpack moving as she walked.

"Someone moved into the village—I'm not sure when this all happened, it was before I lived here for sure. Some of the elders know about it, but I haven't ever really asked. No one really likes to talk about it, aside from people who have had a bit much to drink at the pub, or parents trying to scare their children to bed.

"Anyway, a stranger moved into town. I probably don't need to say how the village doesn't take nicely to folks who aren't from the village. It's a small community, and they like things to be predictable. The people to be predictable. They aren't very nice to folks they don't know.

"This person said they needed work, though, and I guess the person who owned the inn at that time felt sorry for her. She worked in the kitchen, cleaning and washing things, in exchange for a place to stay. She did this for a really long period of time, I've heard. She eventually started getting paid for her work at the hotel and started helping some of the older people tend their gardens and with household chores. One elder in particular needed her help, though I don't remember what her name was. The visitor - they all called her Bezo, an abbreviation for 'visitor' in the old tongue - moved in with the elder, who had taken ill and needed help around the clock.

"Soon after Bezo moved in, the elder passed away. There was a village meeting, and it was determined that Bezo could remain in the elder's house. A number of people did not approve, but those who advocated for her said that Bezo had earned that small house on the edge of town.

"Things went on like that for a while and Bezo settled into life in the village, growing more than enough crops to feed her neighbors and having a number of other skills that benefited the townspeople. Bezo also started attending performances at the theater regularly and acting and performing on stage. She was quite good, so the story goes, and she told a number of her friends in town that she had always dreamed of writing and directing a play. It took some time, but one of her friends recommended her for a weekend theater production, and so Bezo set about writing the play that would be her debut in the village."

I could barely see Henri anymore as the fog had gotten quite thick as we were walking. I asked Henri about it, and she said that the fog rolled off down the hill towards her house most evenings.

"I usually don't use this," Henri said, turning on a small lantern. "It might help tonight, though."

Henri stopped and looked, but the light from the lantern made it difficult to see anything.

"I'm afraid it won't be of much use after all. The light is getting caught in the fog." She extinguished the flame and put it back with her gear.

The sudden absence of light made it impossible to see anything. The horse moved slowly forward, though, and Henri told me to keep an eye on the lichen on her rucksack. I hadn't noticed the small phosphorescent tendrils woven into the seams of the pack, giving off a faint yellow-green light. We continued on, my eyes fixed on the glowing stitches on Henri's back so as to not get lost.

"Anyway, Bezo wrote the play in a few feverish days and started rehearsal as soon it was finished. Everything was fine at first, until some of the actors started telling other people in town that they didn't feel safe, that Bezo's script referenced the old arts, and things that felt like bad magic. Most people wrote it off; the town is still old-fashioned, but they also have an understanding that art can express anger or fear, so most people went along with it. One elder, a gentleman, went to talk to Bezo about the performance and hear her side of the story, but he had a stroke just outside of her door. Everyone in the performance kept up with rehearsals, though, even if they were uncomfortable.

"Though some people refused to see it, others were curious to find out what had caused such a stir in town. This is where it gets difficult to believe, but I'll tell you as others have told me. Everyone was seated in the theater, waiting for the curtains to be drawn. The lights dimmed, and music started, though no one was sure where the music was coming from. The curtains pulled away to reveal the entire cast on stage.

"They were totally motionless, and it took some time before anyone in the audience realized all of the performers were dead. The stage was filled with corpses, all posed in different ways. Some had wings made of wood and cloth shoved into their backs, like giant bat wings. None of the actors had eyes, and all of their mouths were open. Some of the corpses began to move, like automatons, I'm told, but without wires or electricity.

"The first person to tell me this story said that his grandfather was there, and he said it sounded as if they were singing, with their mouths open, but he had no sense of where the music was coming from. Some people actually stayed and watched the corpses move and sing. He also said that Bezo was nowhere to be seen, but a few townspeople said that she might have been killed as well. Others knew that she had done this, using the play as some sort of ritual of dark magic.

"The second time I heard the story, down at the pub, the person said there were pictograms carved all throughout the theater and on the hand-painted sets, but others say that wasn't true. No one ever found out what the play was about. But that's why the theater has been boarded up all this time. No one performs any more, unless it is in the solitude of their own house. Victor's grandfather painted the prayer wheels that cover the building now, you know..."

I was about to remark on this extraordinary tale but all at once I lost sight of Henri's pack. The fog was so dense. I brought Hesperides to a trot, and called out to Henri, but there was no answer. I couldn't have fallen far behind her, but somehow, the horse and I were alone. I strained to see anything in the gloom but the fog was impenetrable.

Suddenly up ahead I saw the flash a pair of red eyes, and whatever they belonged to, they were pacing back and forth, the walk of a predator that knows its prey.

They seemed to be far away, but it was difficult to tell in the fog. A fine mist of rain began to fall, which started to dissipate the fog, and Hesperides began to move away on her own accord. I called out to Henri again, but she did not answer.

The woods filled with low groaning noises. Each moment seemed to push me further and further from an understanding of reality. I felt dizzy and hypnotized. I imagined that branches were cracking overhead in rhythm with Hesperides's gait. I didn't even notice the shade - a hulking presence that was darker than the fog around me - until it had knocked me off the horse.

On the ground I could see the red eyes running towards me. I thought I was about to be attacked by the shade and whatever predator was emerging from the fog, but all at once the dogs, their eyes glowing, leapt out of the fog and surrounded me. They barked and snarled, looking for the presence that had hurt me, and I scrambled to my feet. I searched the ground for a stick or something else to defend myself with and found a stone for each hand.

It wasn't just one shade, though. I counted at least six shadow figures, peeking around the trunks of trees just off the path. I heard a deep droning sound and felt it in my chest. The sound itself made me sleepy, but I pushed on, trying not to listen to the chants of the shadows.

Another flew towards me and I ducked, taking a swing with one of the rocks tight in my fist as it passed above me. I thought I made contact, the skin of my hand feeling some sort of foggy thickness, but it didn't deter the shade, which hid behind a tree after it passed.

I heard Hesperides scream and I looked over to see a shade attached to her strong neck like a leech. I looked around for the dogs, hoping that they'd be able to help, but they were nowhere to be found. The horse jumped and kicked, trying to free itself. I ran to Hesperides and grabbed for the shade, trying to pull it away, but the surface of it was wet and it changed shape whenever I got a hold of it. My hands slipped off, over and over, as the dark ghost fed off of poor Hesperides.

I picked up one of the rocks that I had dropped and used my hands to determine where the thing's head was and swung, trying to swing downward so as to not hurt Hesperides. Before I could strike it a second time, three other shades grabbed my back and dragged me into the forest, hitting my legs and head on trees as they dragged me further from the horse. I heard Hesperides give a loud neigh and then run away at a good pace. I hoped that she had freed herself, even as the shades started to attach themselves to me, lying on the forest floor.

I struggled as much as I could, trying to pry the mouths of these dark creatures from my skin, but I soon gave up. I rested my head on the ground and looked into the woods. I saw four pairs of red glowing eyes slowly approaching, low and ready to strike.

The dogs, which seemed twice as large in the fog and rain, didn't make a noise until they were close enough for me to smell them. Just before they pounced, they let out a reverberating growl that made me tremble, and attacked the shades that were sucking on my skin. With the shades in their jaws, they ripped the monsters from me and tore them with their teeth. The two other dogs had come from the other side and were pulling on one of the shades like a rope, growling and fighting for control, when the shade exploded into a haze of a gelatin-like substance, liquid, and mist. I sat up and watched as the animals devoured the remains of the shades and looked around to find that the woods once again were empty. A sulfurous smell permeated my nose, and I realized it was the dogs, sitting in the ashes of the monsters they had destroyed.

I braced myself on a small tree and stood up, limping from tree to tree to return to the path and see if Hesperides was ok. I got there, the dogs still panting and bloodthirsty, but the horse was gone.

+++

The dogs followed more closely as I came to an intersection in the trail. I was lost, hurt, and had no sense of direction. The dogs stepped onto the path in front of me and walked ahead, looking back to make sure that I was following. I didn't have much choice but to follow them.

I had picked up a walking stick, but it was rotten and didn't last long. I felt like I could still see shades looking out from the trees, but none fully emerged with the dogs by my side. I got off the trail and looked for a sturdier walking stick and saw a light on the trail, slowly coming towards me. It was the same type of light I had seen before, one that shone brightly whether it was day or night.

I hurried back to the trail, and saw Hana. She walked towards me and I heard the repetitive cracks of branches from the wood, a staccato pattern, a marching song given by the trees. All of this, everything I'd been through, was worth this moment, the moment that I'd get to see Hana again.

Her glow was that of lightning bugs, illuminating all the plants of the forest. The shades hiding behind tree trunks vanished and all the leaves and plants turned towards her light as if it was the sun.

But as the light got closer, Hana turned into Jefre, walking alongside Hesperides. The light faded into the night in the woods. It was so clearly her, I told myself. She was there, a beacon, sending me hope. I wasn't disappointed because Jefre and the horse were clearly a message from Hana.

"Jefre?" I said. "Are you real?"

"I've been wondering that myself," he said. "Is any of this real?"

I ignored his question. "How did you get here?" I asked.

"I'm not exactly sure," he answered. I could see the confusion on his face and wondered if I had that look when I arrived. Confusion, bewilderment, and wonder sometimes feel the same.

"I found Hesperides, though," he said. "She's fine."

"How do you know her name?" I stared at him and waited for his response. I had forgotten how beautiful he was, the color of his eyes, and the tone of his skin.

"I don't know that, either," he said. "I'm very confused, and frankly terrified."

"Try not to worry," I said. "You'll get used to this place."

"What *is* this place?"

"I—well I don't have many answers, and even the ones I do have won't satisfy you. Listen, do you remember being on the stage?"

"I think so. I remember something terrible, too—being attacked as we were trying to leave. But here, I'm not injured at all."

"Did you see anyone else there?"

"I didn't see anybody, I don't think. I thought I heard someone, though, aside from you."

I took Hesperides' reins and looked into her eyes. She did indeed look fine, and I found no wounds on her neck where the shade had latched on. I felt a great sense of relief, seeing both Jefre and the horse were okay and knowing they could keep me company through the rest of the night in the woods.

"Did you see Hana?"

"What? Why would she be here, too? Have you seen other people that you know?"

"No, of course not...but I thought I saw Hana in the woods."

I saw strain on Jefre's face. "It was just an illusion, I'm sure of it."

I puffed up my chest, ready to argue, and the sounds of the wood reminded me of how pointless it would be. I had already encountered one terror in the trees, but I was more worried about what made the village lock its gates every night. I exhaled and quietly said that it wasn't an illusion. Jefre didn't respond, and I wasn't sure if he hadn't heard me or was just ignoring me.

"What do we do now?" he said.

I let his question hang in the air as I helped him onto the horse. I touched the tender areas where I'd been attacked by the shades and there was nothing there but soreness and the blunt pain of what would undoubtedly be a bruise tomorrow. I heard a howl in the distance. Jefre heard it, too, and looked to me for answers, but I had none to give him.

+++

Jefre and I, riding Hesperides, followed the dogs through the woods. I still held out hope that they were leading us to Henri's house, or some other place that we might take shelter and safety through the night until dawn.

I told Jefre everything that had happened as we rode. He was polite, but I'm sure he found it difficult to accept. The dogs were excited, following the howls in the night, and ran ahead of us and then returned. Even through our conversations, I could hear the flapping of wings up above us, just like in the Screen. In the wood, though, it made sense; bats or owls, I told myself. It felt natural here and I wasn't afraid, but the sound reminded me of the gnawing of blunt teeth.

When I told Jefre about Hesperides and Victor, it reminded me of what I'd done. A wave of guilt pushed my shoulders down. I stopped short of admitting my own guilt in Victor's death, inferring blame on the director.

"What's wrong?" he asked.

"Nothing. I just...it's been a lot, to be here. But I swear I saw her."

"She's not real." Jefre's voice was sharp, cutting through the night air.

I was taken aback, and angry. But I kept silent and pushed away the negative thoughts as the dogs led us to some path. Something new started growing inside of me, and I wasn't quite sure what it was or how to handle it. The anger towards Jefre and his stupid comment fed whatever it was, though.

"Where are we going anyway?" he asked.

"I don't know," I told him. "The dogs are leading us somewhere."

I felt my hearing going in and out, random noises coming and going; I realized that I was dozing off and was seeing strange things from some other world. Busy city streets flashed to memories of banquet dinners I'd never attended. I saw a scene from a musical which changed to aerial footage of melting glaciers, as if someone was changing the channel rapidly.

"What's wrong?" Jefre asked again.

"Nothing. I'm just tired." Which was true; I was tired of trying to explain things.

I must have dozed off on Hesperides back, but I didn't return to the Screen. I think it was some sort of nightmare or dream; the mixed images continued to change as if I was walking by dioramas in a museum. They couldn't hurt me, that much I understood, but some of the visions were very disturbing, feeding the dark thing that was growing inside of me and feeding off my anger. I saw the stage with corpses fixed in different poses, some with crude wooden and fabric wings that had been driven into their backs, and I remembered Henri's horrific tale. I saw brightly colored patterns and symbols painted in circles that started moving, rotating, and throbbing. I was floating through all of these things, but they were happening at the same time, a paroxysm of images and stories that had, all of the sudden, decided to assault my thinking.

Jefre shook my shoulders. I had no patience for him to ask me if I was o.k. again.

"I think we're here."

I rubbed my eyes and looked at what he was gesturing to. The dogs paced around, anxious for us to enter through the gates. I had a feeling that these gates never closed.

Eight

We stood at the open gates of a village without any sign of life. The fog had cleared and the town stood empty. Some of the buildings had burned while others were old and weathered. All of the buildings had dark holes where their windows had been, looking at us in the night. Jefre walked through the gate first. I tied Hesperides to a post and followed Jefre and the dogs.

The ground was dry and cracked. There were few plants growing except for a few gnarly trees that arose from the derelict houses.

"Perhaps we can find a place to sleep for a few hours, until morning," I said to no one in particular. Jefre had walked down a side street and was out of sight.

It wasn't an exact copy, but the ghost village had some similarities to the hamlet I'd stayed in the night before. There was a large building in the center that looked to be in better shape than most of the other buildings, and a church-like building stood across the overgrown street, matching its height with its bell tower. The church, too, was in respectable shape.

"Jefre? Where are you?"

There was no answer. The dogs walked around as if looking for him. The largest of the animals, that I'd started referring to in my head as Shuck, barked, but there was no response.

I opened the door to the three-story building but refrained from entering. I looked around for Jefre again to see if I could find him.

I closed the door and walked down some type of Main Street. There were plots that looked like they were once used for gardening but were now overgrown brambles. A postage stamp in one corner had wooden graves, many of which had fallen.

The other building's door was open. It looked like a church, I suppose, because of a large black wood-clad tower at its front. I walked over and entered, assuming Jefre had opened the door, but the building was empty. The darkness inside it felt complete, and comforting.

I could hear something, though.

I saw no movement. The noise was peculiar, like footsteps in snow and people talking, but they all seemed distant. I could smell burnt matches, too.

I started seeing things in the shadows. Tentacles of black smoke crawled out from under the pews and rose up, contorting into a phantasm of Hana that sat in the pew awaiting whatever was to come. I walked slowly up the center aisle and watched as curls of dark gas populated the wooden benches with a preternatural congregation. I was about to speak, until someone touched me on the shoulder.

It was Hana, and then it changed to Jefre. I turned back towards the congregation, and the church was empty again.

"You've got to come see this," Jefre said. I rubbed my eyes. I was exhausted.

+++

Jefre hurried me down one of the side streets of the abandoned village. The woods seemed so far away, even though I could see the trees outside the gate, pines whose needles looked blue and black in the gloom. I could also see a waxing moon in the night sky. Aside from a gentle breeze in the pines around the village, the other night sounds were quiet, soft songs of insects.

"I can't believe this, this...tree."

"Where is it?" I said.

"Over here." He stepped between two buildings, pushing a tall desiccated weed out of the way. It was a small passage that opened up into a sort of courtyard. Floating things pushed the air, hovering around a large tree that had dark red bark, the color of dried scabs. The insects, or whatever they were, had five arms like a starfish that held them aloft around the tree. They were luminous, glowing like the lichen stitched into Henri's bag. It was really quite beautiful amidst all of the neglect in the town.

"There," he said. "Look at it."

I turned my gaze to the tree. The trunk had ridges and deep grooves. The color was wrong, but otherwise it looked like a normal tree. I didn't see any leaves in the hundreds of branches, but I hadn't really expected to. The base of the tree was very wide, and the limbs twisted and reached above the houses around it.

But as I looked closer, I saw that there was an opening in the tree. I could see movement inside of the cavity, but I couldn't tell what it was. I stood, listening and looking, and noticed that the movement was in rhythm with my breath, which had slowed in this quiet and strangely peaceful place. One of the glowing insects lowered itself to the height of the hollow and I could see that, in the decayed space of the tree, there were lungs, bloody and exposed, but protected by a ribcage of wood. I was breathing in time with the lungs inside this tree.

"My god," I said. I stepped back, tripping on the cobblestone in the alley, and fell against the side of the house.

Jefre grabbed me, but only after I'd hit my head against one of the old shutters, scraping it against exposed nails and splinters of wood. The dogs, waiting outside of the alley, started barking and my head started bleeding freely, dripping onto my shoulder and down my back.

"Here, use this," Jefre said and handed me his jacket. I put it over the cut to stop the bleeding.

"What is that thing?" I said.

"I don't know. I just know I want to get out of here."

We walked back onto the street to find the dogs pacing and whining, ready to lead us somewhere again.

"Where to now?" I asked the dogs.

I dropped Jefre's jacket at his feet. There was still blood, but I didn't want his help with it, and it would stop sooner or later.

We followed the dogs as they led us back towards the tall building in the middle of town, across from the empty church. I walked up to the building and opened the doors once more. Jefre told me to wait for him, but I didn't listen, and entered with the dogs. I didn't care if Jefre was coming with or not. I felt new enmity flowing through my body, and somehow knew that he was holding me back, keeping me from the meaning of this place. He'd always kept me from Hana, too.

The door to the building stood open and there was light coming from inside.

+++

It was in the center of town, but the shape and stature of the building also reminded me of the old theater with the brightly colored paintings from the other town, the town that had people living in it. Nothing was alive here, except, perhaps, for that breathing tree. Even it lacked healthy growth.

The light fluctuated, growing brighter and then dim, in random patterns. Even when dim, it was very bright in the dark town surrounded by the trees of the woods, and what had been black and dark blue with some moonlight now changed to brighter yellows, greens, and reds the closer I got to the building. I could hear a chorus of voices, singing slowly and more deliberately, the words making sense in a whole new way. The tree stood in my mind's eye as a touchstone for the lyrics, the floating starfish moving with the voices. I felt, despite Jefre's nagging from behind, some great cosmic understanding, even without the wisdom of knowing.

I opened the door further so that I could squeeze through and pulled much harder than necessary, nearly ripping the door off its hinges. While my eyes adjusted, I listened to the voices and heard Hana again. This time, I knew it was her. She was in the old theater, giving off the light, and singing so that I could find her, surrounded by others on stage, singing in unison.

Inside I saw a large room, lined with seats. It was a beautiful room, warm with golden wood and the acoustics of the singers. People sat in the audience, all frozen in the beauty of the performance of Hana and the other singers. Their faces glowed with the light from the stage. I walked around and found an empty seat and sat and listened.

Even in the years that I was her spouse, I knew nothing of being this close to Hana. I felt as though she was singing directly to me. The songs, in this strange place, were as comforting as anything I'd ever experienced.

Jefre interrupted then, grabbing me by the shoulders and telling me that we should leave.

"But she's here, she's singing," I said.

"She's not real," Jefre said and grabbed my arm. I pushed him away and he fell back. No one in the audience moved despite our interruptions. "Look at who you're sitting next to."

I looked over to see a young man watching the opera. He was utterly still, transfixed by the music. As I continued to look at him, though, I realized that his skin was an unnatural color, and his eyes were closed. His skin, stretched taut and ashen, looked as dry as the dirt in the village. What I had mistaken for a slight smile was a death mask, skin mummified and dried so that his lips could never close again, stretched tight over his skull. I looked at the others and saw more desiccated skin revealing slight openings because their skin didn't fit anymore, mouths black without teeth.

At least two hundred mummified audience members.

I stood up and stepped back in disbelief. I led Jefre towards a side door off the stage. Shuck and the other dogs stood by the door and growled, blocking us from exiting. The arias changed, too, and I was drawn up to the stage by Hana's voice. Jefre pleaded with me not to go, but I couldn't resist her. I had to see her. I was meant to be a part of this opera.

+++

I looked into Hana's eyes for the first time since she'd left, and they destroyed me. I was crying, and she caressed the side of my face. She was the only one on stage singing, and it was a lullaby. I could feel my eyelids getting heavy, but I fought sleep. I wanted to be awake and be with her.

Jefre came up on stage and pulled me away from her. "SHE'S...NOT...REAL!"

His anger was astounding. He walked up to Hana and with god-like strength he pulled her right arm and dislodged it from its socket. He pulled her left arm out of her body and threw both arms off the stage. The rest of the choir scattered and the singing stopped.

Hana's face didn't change, maintaining grace and strength, as she always had. I could tell she was thinking about something, and perhaps was about to speak to me, but Jefre grabbed her shoulders and started picking at her neck. I could only see his fingers pulling on something that then came out, an organ of some kind, with veins and viscera around it.

I watched the light in Hana's eyes fade and the rest of the theater went dark.

Blind with anger and tears, I searched the stage for something to hit Jefre with. Near the curtains, I found a thin but sturdy piece of iron, and charged Jefre. He planted his feet and stopped my charge and we stood, equally matched in strength, locked on the stage, my makeshift weapon stuck between us.

We struggled and, as I tried to adjust my stance, Jefre took advantage and pushed me back, knocking over Hana in the process. I heard her whimper in pain, which gave me hope that she might still be saved. I tried to scramble to my feet as I felt Jefre kick me in the ribs, forcing me to drop my weapon.

"She's not real, goddamn it. Look at her! Use your eyes for Christ's sake."

He had his foot on my back, pinning me to the floor. The wound in my head had opened again and blood smeared on the stage as I struggled. I looked over at Hana, lying a few feet away. I looked at her with all of the love that I'd ever felt, wishing I hadn't seen the life leave her beautiful eyes. I wished that none of this had ever happened, that she hadn't disappeared, and that everything was normal. I wanted desperately to be anywhere but here, anywhere I could be with Hana, happy and whole.

And then I saw it, what Jefre had pulled from the back of her head. There was fluid, but it wasn't blood. What I'd seen as veins were wires, and some of them sparked as I lay pinned to the stage. The wires were attached to a small blue plastic case, about the size of deck of cards.

"I've always been patient with you," Jefre said. It was the most patronizing tone I'd ever heard from him and it made me respect him in a new way. "But I've had enough. Hana is not real. We made her, in college. She was a very primitive automaton. Why can't you remember?"

He began crying, but he still scolded me.

"With everything..." he started, and then reconsidered. "We were both interested in the history of them...in college, after we took that class, and we discussed the clockwork monks...why can't you remember? All of this time, I've tried to be patient. I haven't lied to you, but I apparently let it go on too long. I've tried to tell you."

I didn't know how to respond. I didn't understand what he was saying.

"We really need to leave before more bad things happen," he said, lifting his foot off my back. I slowly stood up, grabbing the piece of iron once more.

"I'm sorry I didn't tell you," he said. "I'm sorry I didn't force you to understand that Hana was a complex toy. You just loved her so much. I didn't know how to handle it."

Jefre dropped to his knees and covered his face, giving in to great, heaving sobs. I moved quietly so as not to alarm him as he continued to cry and mutter his false apologies and lies. I grabbed his shoulder and, with strength I didn't know that I had, I swung the piece of metal like a sword at him, missing his body but connecting with his neck.

It wasn't a clean cut, the metal was too thick for that, but it was enough for Jefre to drop to the stage gasping for air as all fluids exited his body. I watched as he died, gasping for air and making horrid choking sounds. I heard movements elsewhere, too; I first looked at Hana to see if she was alive, but she was gone. Nothing remained on stage except Jefre's broken body and dark smears of blood.

I heard clapping. I looked out into the audience and saw, in the dim light of the moon, the audience stand from their seats and clap their dusty hands in some strange ovation of the dead.

+++

I'd always considered myself to be peaceful, avoiding conflict whenever possible, but anger had taken over inside of me. This anger was the real me, inside, who I really was. I felt more comfortable and more honest. I felt like I had spent so much time and energy pretending to be someone else.

At that moment, too, I knew that I wasn't finished. The dead audience had returned to their seats and I could hear the dogs outside the door. I finished the cut on Jefre and grabbed his head and walked out of the theater, back into the desolate pathways between the houses. I caressed Jefre's face and closed his eyelids. Despite all of my anger towards him, I was still saddened by his death. I consoled myself with the thought that he would live on in a different form, somewhere away from this place.

I found the passageway between buildings and walked up to the tree and placed Jefre's head in the crotch of the tree. Blood dripped from his neck into the grooves of the bark. The lungs in the hollow of the tree flushed and took deep breaths, and Jefre's eyes opened. Jefre's head smiled and filled the lungs by breathing through his mouth. The tree, now with Jefre's head, didn't speak, but stretched and craned its new neck and head and gave a breathy, throaty, yet nearly silent laugh. Though I had just placed it there, the head and tree were now one.

I watched as the floating blue starfish landed on the branches of the tree and turned into leaves. Other new growth sprouted as I watched the buildings around the tree renew themselves.

The dogs sat outside the alleyway, resting. Their work was done for the time being.

I walked out of the alley and looked down the crude street. Most of the buildings I could see were still in disrepair, but there was a familiar light coming from the theater where I'd sacrificed my friend. A few other houses had lights on. The city didn't look as run-down as I thought it had when we arrived.

The dogs stayed in the street as I walked back to the theater. I stepped in to see Hana singing again on stage. I sat down, next to one of the other members of the audience, and fell asleep to her aria about the breathing tree.

Nine

As I slept, I felt like I was floating in an abstract space, some-thing like the Screen at the old theater in some distant life. I knew, resting in the theater and listening to the songs being sung in my new world, the ghost town that I would bring back to life, that I would never go back. I had freed myself from that non-place. Images came and went with my eyes closed, floating in and out beside me, but I could never touch them. I could hear Hana and the dryads from the opera in the background, as if I was sleeping lightly, or their songs bled into my quietus. I couldn't see the director, and I wondered if I would ever see her again aside from when she manifested to feed on Victor. But she spoke to me as I floated.

You have found your way, the director said. *I knew what was inside you, what you had hidden for all of these years.*

Starting at my ankles, something crawled up my legs as I floated, activating every nerve; hundreds of insects' featherweight legs climbing on my skin. They crawled over every part of my body and gathered on my head, telling the others *this is the way.*

I tried to brush them away, but they were invisible or immune to my efforts to free myself. The congregation of little beasts on my head and neck bit all at once, jolting me awake.

+++

The theater was empty when I awoke and the stage empty. Sunlight came in through the windows of the theater and I stretched, stood up, and walked outside to the street. In the daylight, the buildings and houses on the main street looked freshly painted and had glass in the windows. Though still empty, the town felt comfortable. I felt compelled to stay in the town, but also knew that this was the place that I could be with Hana again.

I walked down the street and out the gate to find Hesperides. The dogs followed as we galloped down the path towards the other village, scanning the woods for people or things as I rode. The colors of the forest seemed amplified as if it was going to rain. Everything seemed real. The trees whispered to me old forgotten songs and I sang along.

I stopped short of the village and dismounted my horse. I saw Henri, pulling a cart of wood, heading toward the Western gate. A necklace with a large stone attached to it bobbed up and down as she pulled her cart and caught the pale sun that broke through the clouds as I walked out of the woods. I was unsure how to present myself and opted to greet her by shouting her name.

"Hello!" she said. "I lost track of you in the fog last night. Did you find a place to sleep?"

"Yes, I managed, thanks."

"I'd be careful in the village," Henri said, pulling the cart past me and walking towards the gate. "They want to know what happened to Victor. They know you have his horse."

"Oh, I see."

"Where is your friend that was with you last night?" Henri asked.

"We found an old village. The dogs led me to it."

"Huh," Henri said.

"It looks a lot like the one you take wood to, actually, just in a state of disrepair."

"Well," Henri said. "It's good to see you, I've got to make my deliveries."

"Take care," I said. I waited while Henri entered through the gates and, after she'd turned away from the main road, I entered.

People stared at me as I walked through the town. I had no plan before I entered, I'd only thought about what needed to be done for the tree and for Hana in our old but regenerating town. It would be best if I could lead someone outside the gates, but I doubted that would happen very easily.

"Can I help you find something?" A voice interrupted my planning. It was a middle-aged woman walking down the street with a goat on a leash. Her long, braided hair moved slightly as she spoke to me and it looked similar to the braided rope that was tied to her goat.

"Oh, no, thank you. Just looking for some food." I wasn't hungry, but I knew that I should probably eat something while I was here.

"The public house is down the street, can't miss it." The goat started pulling on the rope she had tied around its neck. "You should turn here, though, and see our historic theater. It is really a sight to behold."

"Thank you, I might do that." She walked away, led by the goat.

I didn't turn immediately, but at the following block I did head north to see if I could get a better look at the outside of the theater. I was curious if it was similar to the building I'd watched Hana's performance in.

No matter where I turned, though, I could not find it. The streets didn't make sense anymore. I'd look up and see the top of the theater with its brightly colored signs (which looked like they were moving, spinning, and rotating), so I'd turn down the next street towards the theater only to find that it was gone.

I gave up and headed back towards the main road through town to look for the pub. I walked out at the block that it was on and turned to see that the theater had been back where I'd been walking. I went in and asked for bread and cheese. As I waited, I watched, looking for someone who might not be missed, someone to give to the tree.

My eyes settled on a young man; he was with a group of people in the village, and might have had a few drinks already, early in the morning. He sat with the group but seemed disconnected, and he spent more time looking into his drink than participating in the conversation. His dark hair nearly covered his eyes but his face looked serious and contemplative. I took small bites of bread and watched, from a distance, observing the group and waiting for them to separate. Without the group, he would be an easy gift for the breathing tree.

+++

The man with dark hair left alone and walked down the street. I kept distance and stepped between buildings so as not to be seen, but I lost him soon after he turned off the main road. There were too many people around and I could feel their eyes watching me as I moved through the streets.

I was stopped by some people asking me if I'd seen Victor. While they didn't look any different than anyone else in the town, they gave me a sense of being official representatives of the village.

They escorted me to a town hall and asked me questions about the last time I'd spoken to Victor. I answered them as best as I could, hiding lies amidst truth, and they agreed that I should be forced to stay until this ordeal was sorted out. I told them that I would be happy to stay, but that Victor's horse was in the woods and I should return it to the stables before renting a room.

This satisfied everyone present and Nilson, a bulky man with stern eyes, said that he would fetch the horse with me. He told me, loud enough so the others could hear, that he didn't like what was going on and felt like an abundance of caution was the appropriate course of action.

Nilson and I walked toward Hesperides without a word. The dogs followed us, much to Nilson's dismay. The sun was hidden behind clouds and I could smell rain somewhere in the distance.

"Over here," I said as I pointed to an empty path.

"How much further?"

"Not too far," I told him, but I'm not sure that he bought my lie.

I led Nilson down a path away from the village and away from Hesperides. Sometimes these things present themselves, I said to myself, as we walked. I wondered how long I had before Nilson realized that we were not walking towards the horse.

The thought answered itself as I saw Nilson pick up a large, felled branch, gracefully enough to not cause a stir but obvious to the dogs and me. In some strange sense, I realized that I could sense the things that they comprehended; smells and sights, from their level, popped into my head as matter-of-factly as stepping outside to tell the weather.

I stopped and turned toward Nilson, who had fallen back to pick up the branch and, perhaps, to run back towards town.

"We're almost there," I said, looking at him. He looked intimidated and afraid; it was an odd feeling to cause such fear. Even though I knew that I needed him I didn't have a plan. I had no idea how I was going to kill him. Nilson looked at me, though, as if his fate was sealed.

I took a step towards him and he planted his feet. He raised the stick above his head to strike me but before it came down Shuck had grabbed Nilson's arm with his teeth.

I continued closer as he struggled with the wolfhound, grabbing a stone from the side of the path. Before I could hit him, though, something struck my own head. Blood dripped down my cheek and my whole face burned in pain. I looked around to see who had struck me and I could not see anyone.

I stepped towards Nilson again, who had been wrestled down to the ground by three of the dogs. Again, an attack from an unknown source came through the woods, this time the whistle of a dart that pierced Shuck in the throat. His grip loosened from Nilson's arm and the dog fell to the ground.

Flashes of light and the voice of Henri flooded my mind. I could see her everywhere, moving unnaturally fast, and whispering an old strange dialect. I could not see her standing plainly in the woods, but she was an ambush of many hands and voices.

I got up once more and walked towards Nilson. I couldn't see out of my left eye as blood continued to flood it, but I focused my right eye to see Nilson running back towards town, one arm clutched to his chest, a green-blue light surrounding him. Shuck lay on the path with no breath left in him, but the other three dogs paced back and forth, unsure what was happening. I could smell ash and something burning, their eyes red with anger, and I finally realized what they were—hounds from hell.

I tried to gather myself to get Hesperides and race back to my own village, but something kept my attention. A light floating in the woods, small at first but getting larger and larger until it was very close. Everything smelled of clove and bay laurel, but I couldn't figure what was coming at me, a complex shape of facets and brilliance.

And then the world turned blue-green. I felt like I was trapped in a blanket of the color and tried to claw my way out, pushing aside giant drapes of fabric and only finding more.

I felt something cold touch my face through the fabric and heard Henri's voice again. I tried to grab at whatever was pressed against my eye and cheek, but I could not get it. Henri spoke the same verse over and over, reciting words that turned the cold amulet into searing hot pain that radiated through my head, touched all corners of my skull, and shot scalding misery through my body. I could hear the dogs barking and Henri's chants, but they faded in and out. I thought that I had surely met my end in those conjured materials.

Blunt teeth grabbed the scruff of my neck and pulled me backwards and away from the magical weapon, away from the pain, and into darkness.

+++

I awoke in the evening in a comfortable bed. I could see flames in a fireplace out of the door to the room and Hana walking in front of the fireplace, carrying a tray with water and food. She asked me how I was doing when she entered, and my heart fluttered as if we were meeting again for the first time. I drank the water and told her that I was ok but needed some rest. She agreed and brought a cool wet rag to wash my face. Her actions never seemed mechanical to me. I doubted that Jefre had ever really known Hana and that his little stunt was nothing but a poor illusion. She was real, and I was with her again.

"We need to give more to the tree, otherwise..." she trailed off and looked out the window. It was almost dark, and I understood.

She gave me a crust of bread and I sat up and took a deep breath. Hana seemed to be slowing down herself, having a harder time moving. Her arms and neck showed no signs of Jefre's attack, but she looked weak, moving intentionally with the energy she did have.

There was a knock at the door just as I attempted to stand. Hana opened it to reveal the director, clad in purple wool.

"Hello, Hunter."

Her voice was as I remembered it. I lowered my gaze; I didn't feel fit for the title. My adversaries had created doubt greater than the anger that had brought me to this place.

"Hello," I said.

"Do you see things clearly now? Do you feel your purpose?"

"I think so."

"Her life depends on your work. Everything here depends on your work. Keep that in mind. Without the breathing tree none of this exists."

I swallowed a dry lump and looked at her. She turned towards Hana and touched her face.

"How are you, my dear?" The director smiled and expressed genuine care.

"I'm am weak," Hana said. "He will find more offerings for the tree tonight, though, I am sure. I placed the hand of the villager on the tree as well."

"Very good."

I thought about a way to ask her what had happened, but the words failed me.

"The anger in his heart is strong, but so is his devotion to you," the director told Hana. Hana smiled and took my cup and plate to the small table, tidying up.

"Have you seen the building in the village with the brightly colored paintings on the outside?" the director asked. "That is my theater, my place of worship. There are members of our family trapped in there with those signs. They need to come home to me, so that I can build a new place of worship here."

I nodded.

"You'll need these glasses. I can't tell you how they work, but they will, I am sure of it." She blew a kiss to Hana and laid the glasses on the table next to the dishes and walked out the door.

I was tired, but able to stand on my own. For Hana, I would do what was needed. I grabbed the glasses and smiled at Hana, and I told her that I would return before morning.

Ten

With the glasses in my pocket, Hesperides, the hounds, and I raced to the village, stopping before we could be seen from the woods. There were no towers, but I guessed that the towns-people would be on high alert after Nilson's return, apparently missing at least one hand. I took Hesperides around a bend in the path that led to town, well into the woods so that he wouldn't be found until I returned.

I had an intense understanding of the woods. I don't know where it came from, but I understood the layout and where things were. I knew there was a weak spot in the fence around the town. The insects and night-birds sang in agreement as I made my way through the trees. I knew that there were other villages nearer than I'd previously imagined. Others for the breathing tree.

I felt the slope of the ground and avoided obstacles without seeing them in the dark of the wood. One of the dogs had re-mained with Hesperides but the other two walked by my side.

I could see through the trees that there were two armed villagers, both carrying large weapons, standing outside the gate.

They didn't seem to notice me as I walked through the woods and found the spot - a series of rotted-out fence posts - that would allow me entrance, undetected.

The planks of wood moved easily, and I slid in. The dogs followed, entering the village for the first time since they'd joined me, and we walked between the buildings, jumping from shadow to shadow. There were lanterns on each of the street corners, but the streets were empty. While there were a few lights on in the small houses lining the streets, most of the windows were dark as well.

I stopped to put on the glasses and stepped out into the light, nearly in sight of someone patrolling the streets. I saw children in one of the homes, looking out the window, unsure of what they were looking for. We stayed in the shadows until they left, though, just to be sure that we were not seen.

With the theater in sight, I heard the sound of boots walking down one of the side streets, and looked to find cover nearby. Behind a row of hedges, the dogs and I remained still, hoping to be undiscovered. There were three people walking past us, talking in hushed tones. One of them was Henri the woodcutter. She was far more than an ordinary woodcutter, of course; a person of cunning and one sensitive to her surroundings.

"Do you think he'll come back?" a woman asked.

"I don't know," Henri answered.

"And that thing you saw...the woman in purple. Do you think it's really her? Do you think she's still here?"

"I don't know," Henri repeated. "I don't even know if it was a woman, honestly..." Henri's voice trailed off as they walked around the corner.

I rose from the bushes after a few moments of silence and looked towards the theater. The color had drained from the paintings and the outside of it appeared the same drab wood of the rest of the buildings. I lifted the heavy glasses off my eyes to look at the theater without them and it disappeared, moving three blocks over and brightly painted again. The glasses had a dial on the side, reminding me of the heavy machines at the ophthalmologist's office, and I turned it a few clicks to see how things changed. As long as the glasses were on, the theater was there, a block away from our hiding spot.

No one guarded the theater. This was surprising at first, until I reasoned that the paintings - the intricate, colorful, and abstract hex signs - had provided all the protection that the townspeople thought was necessary.

I walked in the shadows around the back to see if this theater had a corresponding side entrance to my own building, and I found one. I walked up to the door, which was locked, and used a rock to break the glass, reaching inside to unlock the door.

The noise of breaking glass had drawn attention, though. The dogs started growling as people ran from different directions. I opened the door and entered the theater, in complete darkness. I heard the dogs outside, barking, and chasing the townspeople. I knew that I didn't have much time, and I didn't really know what I was supposed to do, now that I was here.

I could see that the seats were empty. I made my way up to the stage and found the switch for the stage lights and turned them on. The stage was still filled with the corpses of the actors from the story that Henri told me, and the corpses that I had hallucinated so many years ago. Threads of disorientation ran through me as I realized that I'd been here before, or seen this tableau vivant when I was blind, in a phantom vision.

Though they appeared to be dead, their skin still had pigment, and their heads turned as I paced across the stage and formed a plan in my head. Wings made of wood and fabric protruded from the backs of a few of the actors. Some faces had paint and, though their eyes were closed, I swore I could see them breathing. I heard one of the dogs howl in pain outside and I made the decision to break open the front doors and attempt my escape.

Henri's voice entered into the theater, but again, I could not see her. Her words confused me, something like the arias that I thought I had remembered, but the words were all wrong. I unlatched the main entrance to the theater and threw open the doors to see six townspeople with weapons drawn, ready to strike.

I felt a greater force behind me, though, as the wraiths animated and exploded off the stage. They rushed towards the exit and flew forcefully through the open doors. Those with weapons outside the theater tumbled and fell, unable to keep their footing in the attack.

One of the actors with handmade wings pulled me from the building and we flew above the houses. I could see one of the dogs trailing us in the streets. Townspeople, with torches and weapons, followed behind, but had little hope of catching us soaring above the town. The last thing I saw was the gate being opened and the villagers watching us fly away. Their faces were blank, lit only by the torches.

+++

Hesperides and her guard joined the other dogs, though one was having a hard time keeping up. The winged revenant lowered me to Hesperides' back. The hunting party was complete, and we tore through the woods, looking for our next quarry.

We arrived at a cluster of houses situated on a broad grassland a few hours later. Lights burned in the structures even though it was full darkness. Standing near the woods, Hesperides stomped impatiently, and I looked at what we'd become—the remaining dogs with glowing red eyes and smoldering hair, and the actors, the director's brethren, enlisted after their long imprisonment, ready to follow.

Three people emerged from the houses with torches and weapons, but we made quick work of them. In one of the homes I found a large woven sack and, filling it with parts of the dead, mounted it on Hesperides. We rode through the woods and were home before morning.

Others, perhaps the director's brethren, had been adding to the breathing tree in my absence. I attached the appendages and mounted the heads into the tree and watched as the blood ran through the cragged bark and filled the tree with life. Dozens of eyes looked out at me below the tree; what had been amputated was now rejoined with the flesh of the tree and the heads craned and looked at the glory of its body. Hands grew from branches and fingers moved, enchanting the air around the tree. Limbs had been planted in the ground, feeding its roots. It was a holy sight, something I could have never imagined.

The village, renewed and expanding, was filled with the brethren. Though they didn't speak, they had other ways of communicating because their movements were coordinated, human, and orderly. I realized that they existed on some other plane, not quite human nor dead.

I walked into the house that I knew was mine, knowing that Hana was inside, and removed my clothes and slept.

+++

I awoke in the Screen. Its walls, which I thought had been made of wood, were slick like vinyl. There was nothing in the space except for me and my cane. The door that Jefre and I had attempted to exit was gone. Hana was nowhere. I screamed and thrashed, looking for things to hit or pull, though I knew there was nothing around me but emptiness.

"Now, now. You needn't be aggressive. Please calm yourself." The director's voice was soothing, but the anger, from deep inside me, was difficult to control.

"I want to go back, right now."

"We need to talk first," she said. "We need to come to an agreement."

"Anything. I'll do anything."

"I'm sure you would. But I'm not one to let people agree to things based on simple emotional responses. I need more than that. I need you to agree to...the complexities of this situation."

"Tell me, I will agree to them."

"You realize that you will never come back here, or to your old life."

"Yes. What else?"

"You will have to continue to build the town, giving the tree what it needs. You will need to destroy lives for it to live."

"I understand," I said. I had calmed down some, though my breath was still shallow and fast.

"And you must know that if you die in the woods your life will end, with no hope of any sort of afterlife."

"Agreed."

"I will not always be able to protect you, from the wood-cutter, or others."

"There are others?"

"Yes, of course. There are always others. I've attracted quite a few adversaries over time. That's part of why I need you, huntsman." She caressed the side of my face as she spoke.

"Why else do you need me?"

"Now, here, finally, a good question. You are a part of a greater plan, as I am sure you now realize. There are things that are difficult to explain, but let it be said that I am working towards the reckoning of the non-believers. I have used the theater as a sort of chapel, giving alms; but through these theaters, no matter where or when they exist, it is not enough."

"What more do you need?" I asked.

"I need places of invocation and approbation. You must profess of my power, through your actions. The breathing tree is a testament to my power, the town is ours to transmit our message of mystery. There will be times of misery, death, and absence. Voids that are full and what was rational made strange. All of these things, and more, will bring a new reality to these worlds. A reality where the living and the dead are together, an audience for my awesome power."

Any anger that was left turned into confusion. I had little idea what she was talking about, but I knew that it was beyond my understanding, and for my purposes, beside the point. "Whatever you require," I said. "I just want to be back with Hana."

"There is one more part of our agreement," she said. "Hana is beyond your comprehension—and even mine. A spirit, of sorts, one that lives with trees. She is not under my control..."

"Am I under your control?"

"No, not in a literal sense. All of this...world, the woods...is set up for you to *understand* your nature. You can choose to stay here or return to the woods. What you've been calling the brethren are, to a large degree, under my control. Though I have to state that I find that term offensive, given that they are both men and women.

"They will help you; they thrive when the breathing tree thrives. They were trapped in that theater for so long.... In any event, Hana is of a tree. A walnut tree, to be precise. I was able to invite her into the woods through a walnut tree. She has her own powers and is a timeless one; I cannot guarantee that she will remain with you until your death."

"What do you mean?"

"She may choose to leave, but you are still bound by our agreement, regardless of what Hana decides."

"Jefre said something, the reason I killed him...I mean...I don't know. Is Hana real?"

"Oh, yes. She's very real. I will say, though, that to Jefre, she was never real, due to a limitation of his own mind, if you will, a limitation of what he could accept as reality. He always thought she was an automaton, so that's what she was to him."

"I'm not sure I understand."

"Nor do you need to."

"May I return, then? To my new—"

"It is not new, it has always been a part of your reality. You just did not have access to it before now; you had limited yourself just as Jefre had."

"O.k. May I return, then?"

"There is one last thing, hunter."

"What is it?"

"In death…I have no control over what happens to you. What will happen and where you will go after your death, wherever you find yourself, I will have no control over. I'll have no spiritual dealings with you."

"Fine. I'd like to return now."

Eleven

I awoke to Hana moving in our house. It was nearly dark again. I drank water and ate some bread and cheese that Hana had set out on the table, and got dressed.

Hana sang a song about harvesting crops and the goodness of the earth. I was pleased to hear her singing again. She looked healthy, as I remembered her, when we'd first met.

I kissed her forehead before leaving and told her I would be back soon.

The town outside was alive. There were still derelict buildings on the outskirts of town, but I could see tall plants growing in lots next to them and imagined that the soil was providing vegetables and grains for us. I wasn't sure if the brethren ate, but the village felt full of life.

I walked down the streets and surveyed what had changed since yesterday. Houses had been repaired and plants grew between the houses and streets. Trees sprouted up in unusual places, too; in the middle of the streets, next to houses, and proliferated the town. Though they were small, the rough bark and reaching branches reminded me of the breathing tree, and I wondered if these were offspring.

What had been burnt, black, and dried now shone with a luster. Glass was clean and clear, wood was newly milled and polished. I saw a newly painted sign by the gate giving the town its name: Lazarus.

I ended up at the theater and walked in to see two of the brethren, both females with wings, performing together for the audience. It was a remarkable reenactment of their escape from the theater as far as I could tell, and there was a person, sitting on a horse, made from straw and sewn fabric; I assumed that it was a representation of me. I felt uneasy being a part of the lore that was being performed on that stage and could only think of my own dramas that had unfolded there just a short day before.

Mythology had formed and changed within a few days. All of the people and places that were dead had a new sort of life, one that came with its own histories and memories. Time meant so little to me now in this place where there was no finality in death.

The audience in the theater was remarkable. Seeing a theater full of dried, animate humans was shocking enough, but to look at them now and see that their skin was no longer leathery and to see something human in their eyes was beyond amazement. Their flesh had pigmentation; their bodies had breath. Their mouths were slightly off, still not fully closing the gaps, but their skin was not as dry as before. The breathing tree was a wonder, fueling life all around me in the village.

The dogs were outside waiting when I exited the theater, and I knew it was time to go. Four brethren, standing by Hesperides, waited for the evening's hunt.

+++

As the breathing tree grew, so did my understanding of the woods. Minutes might have been days as time had less meaning in Lazarus, and I knew each tree in the forest as if they were geographic markers.

The woods, now fully cartographically represented in my mind, was full of other villages and hamlets. Lazarus was not accessible to most people walking in the woods, however. I was sure that stories were told about the ghost village, but few would ever see it.

Hesperides, the dogs, and I kept a moderate pace through the woods, heading towards another gathering of houses that I understood to be a short distance from the overlook that Victor had led me to. I could hear the brethren following through the woods close behind us. The dogs knew our destination and their fur had already started smoldering, giving off the faint odor of cinders as we approached the three houses clustered around a magnificent black walnut tree. Barns and outbuildings dotted the land that had been cleared for crops, providing cover for our hunt.

Though it was early in the evening, there was only a single lantern burning inside one of the houses. From the woods, we saw no movement, and I made the decision to wait and watch before we entered.

Aside from a large bird that must have been perched in the walnut tree, I saw no movement. The dogs were getting restless, and the brethren stood, waiting for my signal. The owl was an omen, I thought, as I watched it swoop into the field.

"Slowly," I said, and we all walked towards the houses.

Something was not right in the village; I couldn't exactly place it, but I had reservations as soon as we started towards the buildings. Everything was empty, though. No animals in the barns and the houses were empty, even though there were vegetables and bread on the table of the house with the lantern.

The dogs started barking outside at the base of the tree. I walked outside to watch the brethren effortlessly scale it, though I knew not what they were chasing after. I tried to calm the dogs, but their eyes turned to fiery red and their paw prints in the dusty ground smoldered as they paced and barked at the base of the tree.

I stood, looking up into the lower branches of the tree, trying to locate the brethren, but I could only hear them climbing amongst the limbs and leaves. The dogs had disappeared, turning into black smoke; I could hear them barking and could see their red eyes amidst the clouds of smog moving around the base of the tree. I tried not to panic. A low, thunder-like sound came from the woods around the hamlet; it got deeper and louder as I tried to make sense of what was happening.

I readied my weapon and stood by the tree.

What came out of the woods was not what I had expected. Three figures, one with a limp and missing a hand, strode towards the houses with confidence. There was a deep, low sound emanating around them that filled my head and made it difficult to think. With my simple iron blade, I prepared for their arrival.

The dogs had also sensed the beings coming from the forest. I noticed that one of the figures swung something overhead; it looked as though it could be some sort of weapon, but there was no way that it could reach me, so I just watched the figures as they approached. Still in the form of smoke and hellfire, the dogs charged the figures walking towards us.

As soon as the trail of the dogs' smoke and ash got near the figures - who I could now make out plainly as Henri, Nilson, and another of the villagers - the smoke disappeared, as if their fire had been extinguished. I could still hear the dogs barking, but the beasts were not visible as the three continued towards me.

The sound was a bullroarer. The small piece of wood spun above the heads of the figures as they approached the tree, providing some sort of shield, and scaring off the brethren.

+++

"There is no one here," Henri said. "We've moved them to our village."

"I'm sure we'll find another place," I said. "Perhaps, now that you are here, your village is not so well protected?"

"We won't let you past us."

I looked around. Others had come from the woods and surrounded the buildings. Most of the people had torches, but some held bows and arrows pointed towards me.

I stepped out from the shadows and noticed the full moon. I watched Henri as she stopped by one of the buildings. I knew that it would be difficult to outrun arrows, but whatever her abilities were, I also knew that I had a better chance running any other direction.

As I tried to move quietly to one side of the tree, the brethren up in the tree provided the distraction that I needed for escape. They let out a guttural scream as they descended from the high branches and knocked down the people of the village. One landed on Nilson who struggled as Henri and their companion tried to get him off. The sound of the bullroarer stopped suddenly. Arrows flew everywhere and stuck in the tree and the houses around it.

I heard the dogs barking again and saw, swirling around the edges of the buildings, thick black smoke with red eyes and white teeth. They made quick work of the people holding torches, which fell to the ground and burned until the dry grass and plants around the houses caught fire.

I stepped away from the tree and started walking towards one of the houses and was surprised to see villagers with weapons pointed towards me as they came out of hiding in the houses. Pinned near the roots of the walnut tree, I looked for escape as more people came out of the houses and barns, all with weapons drawn towards me.

Before anyone could use their weapons the tree roots near me burst out of the ground and wrapped around me. I tried to move, tried to escape, but the thick roots of the tree had braided around my abdomen and limbs. The tree pulled me towards its base and the villagers, so intent on killing me moments before, watched in horror. Arrows flew and flames ravaged the houses. I reached up as my body plunged into the soil around the tree.

The roots moved me through, hugging my body, as I was pulled into the maze of buried appendages. Nestled below the tree, wrapped in cellulose, I watched worms and larvae squirm and writhe, attentive only to their own needs. The roots hummed and intonated, and I lost consciousness, expecting death.

+++

It did not come.

I woke up in bed, in the village, in the theater. I adjusted and realized that I was bandaged up. Though I could feel it and the sensation of moving my body with it, my right arm was gone, and my shoulder was covered in gauze.

Hana was there but she looked weak. Any pleasantness in Lazarus had faded and the building looked dull, the edges of things blurry. It was still night out, or perhaps I had been gone for an entire day and night had come again.

"I think he will be ok," Hana said. I hadn't seen the other person in the room, but Henri sat at our table, drinking tea. She looked tired; there was dirt and blood and little flecks of color on her clothes.

"I'm glad," Henri said in a flat voice. "They ripped him from the tree...I couldn't stop them."

"They are not very sophisticated," Hana said.

"And you? What are you here?"

"That is a difficult question to answer," Hana said. "I love him; this is one of my stories."

"Stories...what do you mean?"

"We are ageless, infinite I guess," Hana said. I stayed still so that I could listen further. I wasn't sure that I wanted to hear it, but I needed to.

"I have been here for a long time," Henri said. "We all will die, though."

"I am different. I am...I was born of a tree and will always be connected to the tree."

Something sunk in at this moment; the weight of everything fell on me hard and kept me down on our bed. The weight of everything, my part in this new lore, broke me. I had always treated Jefre and Hana poorly, living as though I was owed something, not understanding how much they gave to me. In this place, I embraced some monstrosity that was a part of me. Lazarus, which would now die again, was my fitting home. I tried to cry quietly.

"You're awake," Henri said.

I cleared my throat and shifted up in bed as well as I could.

"How are you feeling?"

I didn't know what to say; a quiet, low grumble exited my mouth. I stared at the wall, holding back more tears.

"Well, you should be fine here, for the time being."

Turning to look at Henri, I could see in her eyes that she meant me no harm. Her goal had always been to prevent harm.

"How did you get here?" I asked, and cleared my throat again, fighting against the hoarseness.

"Your horse. I rode with you; you were delirious when they pulled you from the tree."

"From the roots?"

"From the trunk. The tree had opened up somehow and...I don't know what happened. The brethren tried to pull you out."

"Were others harmed?"

"One of the townspeople was hit by an arrow, but she'll survive. The brethren were beheaded, but I'm not sure..."

She didn't need to finish, I understood. Things that aren't exactly alive or dead don't have tidy endings. "Did they return here?"

"They are gone from here," Hana answered.

I tried to sit up, but the room spun and I lay back down.

"You'll be safe here," Henri said, and her words trailed into my unconsciousness as I fell asleep again.

Twelve

What you will one day remember is that I was real and that I was imagined.

I don't expect you to understand everything, but Jefre was correct, and you were correct.

Things and beings and time and space are often one and nothing. I will always be here and there is nothing I can do to curse you with that life. I always knew that one day you would die and return to that flat black space I heard you speak of in your dreams.

You might still hear me sing, in the wind through trees, or in other empty voices that inherit all things.

The breathing tree, that monstrosity made by the director, is slowly dying. I can hear it moaning day and night and its breath is wheezy and dry. It must die again, and I must go.

You will remain here, in this place. Everyone in this ghost village has returned to the dead and the missing. You will be alone here, guarded by new paintings of brilliant colors.

I know you have always wanted to be with me, but I must go now, for good. Perhaps you didn't understand the anger and defiance that's been building in your life since you were much younger.

Our worlds will not intersect again and you will hear no more of the songs in the woods. Goodbye, dear Nathaniel. I wish for you honest rest.

+++

I can see outside, and the buildings have fallen apart again, Lazarus returning to its former dereliction. I know what is outside of my house, what is keeping me in. Henri is someone of multiple talents, I now realize, and the one who paints the brightly colored wheels of confinement. I can see outside, see everything, but here I remain.

I can walk out the door and I end up directly in the same room I exited. I can do it all day and still will never leave the house. Climbing through a window produces the same results.

Hana is gone. I expected it, I think, I deserve to be alone.

I feel lost, which is the strangest part of all of this.

I have no hunger, and I do not seem to be starving.

I thought that the Screen was some sort of purgatory, but I believe that I have found something much more real.

I do not know if I will be like the brethren, somewhere between living and dead, or if I have achieved some sort of immortality, or if it is a curse from Hana or Henri. I do not know what will happen if someone frees me from the binding paintings that I see in my dreams at night.

+++

At an altar, in the wood, four hamadryads are singing:

I do not envy them, not one bit. Their lives are filled with tragedy.

I loved one once, in a dream, or something like it. He was a kind human at first, but his heart was blank and empty.

What a pity!

Yes, indeed.

The trees are always here, we are always here. They see things as so long, lasting forever, and only in their sense of time. They have no concept of what time really is.

Yes, indeed!

Shall we perform the ritual?

Have we not already started?

Many thanks to my spouse Amy and my children Hazel and Sam for their support. Thanks also to my parents and brother. My mother instilled the importance of reading when I was young and for that I am eternally grateful, gladly passing on the beauty of reading to my own children. Though my father passed away in 2016, his memory lives on, and his brothers and sisters are the greatest story tellers I've ever known.

This book would not be possible without the amazing talents of Catherine Knepper. In 2020 I decided that I wanted to write stories and her editing has taught me a great deal about writing.

Thanks, also, to Neal Vandenbergh for use of his amazing drawing for the cover.

This story wouldn't exist without Ethel Smyth's opera *Der Wald* and E.T.A. Hoffmann's short story "The Sandman." Both of these works haunt me, even though I can only read stories about the original opera.

Benjamin Gardner is an artist and writer living in Bloomington, Indiana. His short fiction has been included in anthologies and zines and he serves as co-owner and editor of Theurgical Studies Press, a small press dedicated to limited edition risograph zines. He has released two albums through Neverwood Records as Asurta. His project Adoricst Books explores new ways to tell stories through words and images and includes The Trailer on Quiet Lake, a novel published through Substack. You can find out more information about the author at benjaminagardner.com.